I0453792

TEACH ME TO PREY

SAMANTHA JACOBEY

Lavish
Publishing LLC

This book is a work of fiction. The characters, incidents, and dialogue are drawn from the author's imagination and are not to be construed as real. Any resemblance to actual events or persons, living or dead, is entirely coincidental.

TEACH ME TO PREY. Copyright 2015 ©

All rights reserved under International and Pan-American Copyright Conventions. By payment of the required fees, you have been granted the non-exclusive, non-transferable right to access and read the text of this e-book on-screen. No part of this text may be reproduced, transmitted, down-loaded, decompiled, reverse engineered, or stored in or introduced into any information storage and retrieval system, in any form or by any means, whether electronic or mechanical, now known or hereinafter invented, without the express written permission of Lavish Publishing, LLC.

First Edition

All Rights Reserved

Published in the United States by Lavish Publishing, LLC, Midland, TX

Cover designed by WYCKED INK

Images: ADOBE STOCK

Paperback Edition

ISBN: 9780692476215

www.LavishPublishing.com

Contents

Prologue

REBECCA STEWART PLACED her elbows on the table, laying her head in her hands, "I need a cigarette."

"You know, smoking is bad for someone in your condition," Detective Browning stated bluntly. Pulling the pack out of his pocket, he dropped it on the flat surface between them.

"I don't give a fuck what's bad for me," she cut her eyes up at him without lifting her face. When he placed the lighter on top of the box, she reached for the carton and removed one. Her hand shook, causing the little flame to dance as she inhaled. The end of the white paper cylinder glowed bright red for a moment, and she exhaled a thick cloud, then licked her lips. "Thank you."

"Yeah," he grimaced, "Let's get back to it."

"Jesus Christ," she leaned back in the stiff wooden chair, "I already told you everything."

"Then you'll tell me again," he growled, running a hand through his silvery hair. "Start at the beginning. Tell me about the day you met Jason."

Her eyes instantly glazed, and Becky could hear the tone of

the bell that the school used to signal class changes. "It was the first day of school," she admitted quietly. "He was just a kid. Just one of the hundred and fifty students on my roster."

Her mind trapped in the past, her heart began to pound heavily against her ribs. *I needed to learn their names,* she recalled. "We played a game that day; only there weren't any winners. I wanted to know who they were and something about them." She sighed loudly. "One of the veteran teachers told me that would be a good way to get the upper hand quickly."

"This was your first year to teach?"

"No," she took a long drag, blowing out loudly and staring at the mirror that covered the wall behind him. "I taught ninth grade for six years; I hated it. The kids were loud and obnoxious. Moving to the senior course was my last option; if I couldn't cut it there, I'd have to leave the profession."

"Alright; so you wanted to learn about them. What did you learn about Jason," his voice dropped to a practiced calm, drawing her out.

Becky sneered, "You're really good at this."

"Good at what?" he pulled out the seat across from her and sank easily into it.

"This... thing. Manipulating people," she held the nasty grin. "I wasn't ever good at it. I'm too nerdy; too... different."

"Ok," he agreed, placing the pack of smokes back into his jacket and sliding the ashtray closer to her. Focusing on the inch of burnt material threatening to drop off at any moment, he nodded, "It's ok, Becky. Start again. Tell me what you remember, and maybe I can help you."

Staring at him, blinking her large brown eyes slowly, she chuckled, "Man, I doubt that. I messed up somewhere. Made a bad choice, and I'll be damned if I can figure out which one. And now I'm sitting here, talking to you; in the middle of a murder investigation." She would have cried again at the thought of it, but after so many hours, all she felt was numb.

"Yes, you're talking to me, and don't worry about the investigation; it will take care of itself. Focus on the truth. This is your chance to tell me your side, and maybe do away with some of those poor choices. So, what is it you have to say?"

ONE

Nervous Wreck

"Jesus Christ," Becky mumbled to herself, wiping anxiously at her blouse with a paper towel. "First fucking day of school, and I look like shit." Licking a napkin, she applied it to her full round breast, working desperately to remove the stain from the white shirt.

Seeing that it was no use, she darted out into the hall and used her key to open the door directly across from hers. "Help!" she called loudly to the woman seated at the desk.

Glancing over with a smile, Anna Marshall waved her into the tidy room, "What's up?" Standing, her tailored navy blue pantsuit stood out sharply.

Staring at her for a moment, Rebecca's jaw hung open before she breathed, "You look... stunning. So... professional," and she raised her arms, silently indicating the hot mess that she represented.

"Thanks," the short blonde stepped forward, her heels clicking against the tile floor. "It helps to maintain the distance right from the start. I'm the teacher," she placed her hand flat against her perky bosom, "And they are the students," she wafted it at the empty desks. "Now, what is it that you need?"

"I spilled my coffee on myself, and I need a way to cover it," the younger woman stammered.

"Hmm," Anna studied her more closely, "Well, I would loan you my sweater, but obviously it's not going to fit."

Gaping at her, Becky briefly considered if that were some kind of jab. A good five inches taller, she also outweighed the other woman by at least fifty pounds. Although not qualifying as fat, Rebecca sported a hefty rack that meant the two of them would never share clothing; "Obviously," she agreed quietly.

"Go down the hall and see if Glenda Pritchard has a sweater or jacket that you can borrow. Her room is on the other end."

"Yeah, I know where she is," the girl frowned at the thought of the prudish spinster.

"Well, there you go," the petite woman placed her fingers gently on her arm, indicating the door with the other hand, "I'm sure she can help you out."

Leaving the room dejectedly, Becky stomped down the corridor and knocked on the wide wooden entrance, not daring to let herself in. Of all the teachers she had met at her new campus, Ms. Pritchard had to be her least favorite. Drawing a deep breath, she steeled herself to face the grey-haired old biddy; "Hi."

"Yes?" cool blue eyes glared at her.

"I've had a little accident," she indicated the spot she wanted desperately to cover, "And I was hoping you might have a sweater I could borrow."

Her pudgy lips pursed, the older woman responded by turning to the floor-to-ceiling cabinet next to her. Removing a shabby, black button-down, she offered it in a begrudging manner; "Return it."

"Yes, ma'am," Becky replied softly, taking the coarse and worn garment and scurrying back to her haven. Moving to her own locker, she opened the door and slipped her arms into the sleeves. Her fingers trembling, she fixed the buttons and inspected herself in the mirror. *Well, shit.*

The older woman much larger in size, the covering clearly did not belong to her. A tone sounded, and the girl jumped, "It'll have to do. I either get to wear a large brown mark on my tit all day, or cover it with this… hideous thing." Opting for the latter, she closed the cupboard and moved to the door, ready to greet her students for their first day of class.

Eight hours later, Becky stood at her desk, staring down at her notes. All day, every period, she had gone through the roster, placing the students onto a blank seating chart according to where they had chosen to sit. In turns, they had all given their names, as well as what they liked to be called.

Under the advice of her mentor, Bill Carver, she had asked each one what they did after school, or what activities they liked to take part in. At first, she had doubted that it would be a useful exercise, but studying their responses at the moment, she could see that a large percentage were employed. *No wonder he told me to ask; knowing what they face when they leave my classroom could actually help me a lot.*

Looking up when her door opened unexpectedly, she found herself face to face with Ms. Prude herself. Seeing that she held her hand extended towards her, Becky deduced the older woman had come for her belonging. Slipping off the ebony sweater, she smiled, "Thank you. It was most helpful."

Snatching the garment, the older woman looked her up and down, then grunted, "You'd do well to put a change of clothes in your cabinet." Turning her back, she sauntered out without another word.

Staring after her, a forlorn feeling eked its way into her chest. Rebecca had come to Central High out of desperation. She had not fared well in her previous assignment, and had found herself under an improvement plan for the last two years.

Making the move to the larger campus, she had accepted the position working with seniors in hope of salvaging her career.

Shifting her gaze back to the pages covered in names and stories, she sighed loudly, "Nine months. Nine little months, and we tackle them one day at a time."

Taking a seat in the stiff wooden chair, she pulled out a fresh set of charts to begin arranging the classes into a more suitable pattern. Above all else, she wanted to be prepared for the challenges that managing a classroom brings, and this was the first step.

A smart lady, Rebecca Stewart hadn't taught this age group before, but she knew letting them make the rules would be a bad idea. She needed to have a plan, and allowing them to sit with their friends would be a disruption she needed to avoid. *Yup; one day... one step at a time.*

Rock Along

"So," Detective Browning spoke, drawing the young woman across from him back to the present, "What did you write on that paper about Jason Truitt?"

Rebecca wrinkled her nose, her eyes squinting in an effort to read the page. "He had a group of friends in the class; they all sat together, and were overly talkative from day one. I don't remember if that was the day he told me he had a job, but at some point I found out where he worked."

"At HH?"

"Yeah, that's where he worked," she sighed. "Only, it didn't matter to me back then. Not like that. Back then, he was one of the kids in my class, and I treated them all the same, regardless."

"Ok, so what did you do about their talking?"

"I moved them around. But that was a challenging class right from the start; thirty four kids and they had been friends from grade school. Sitting them next to people they wouldn't talk to had been virtually impossible," the girl clicked her tongue. "After the first six weeks, I realized that their behavior wasn't really hurting them, so I let it go, and relaxed more."

"You let your boundaries down," he fished calmly.

Cutting him a cold glare, she hissed, "I didn't do anything wrong. I remained a professional for the entire year; those boys are the ones who caused this. They are the ones who were responsible."

"Ah," he waggled an extended digit at her, "But you claimed you didn't know that at the time."

"No, I didn't," she acquiesced with a small shake of her head, "But I did loosen my grip on them a little. Only one kid failed the first six weeks in that class, so obviously they got their shit done, and that's all I cared about."

"Why was that important?"

"Because," she sneered; "If you have too many students failing your classes, it looks bad. Administration wants to know what you're doing wrong, so you have to be aware of your numbers."

"That sounds a little odd," he grimaced, "It's not you turning in the work; it's them."

"Yeah, I know. Tell that to downtown," she waved a hand angrily. "That aside, I wanted them all to learn; that's the whole reason we're there. If they were getting good grades, we were meeting both of those goals, so I let things rock along. If we finished early, I let them talk and visit; that was good incentive for them to get their assignments done and not give me grief when we had work to do. That's what I mean by relaxed; I let them have free time."

"I see," he leaned back in his chair. "And what did they talk about during their free time?"

"Well, it depended," she rolled her eyes, thinking about the subgroups of her largest class. "There was a group of four or five girls in there who all took cosmetology. They liked to sit together and talk about hair and nails and makeup."

"And you enjoyed visiting with them about those things?"

Staring at his hands, she admired his deep-brown flesh. *I bet he's hispanic; even with the name Browning, he doesn't look white.* The idea brought to mind her English language learners and their special needs for a moment. *So many different types of kids; so many things to consider.* "No," she clipped, then sighed loudly, "I'm not really a girly girl, so that stuff bored me to tears."

"So which group did you end up talking to?"

Hesitating a moment longer, she flicked her gaze up to meet his. "Jason and his friends talked about games, computers and stuff like that. That's what interested me.. that's the group I liked to listen to, but I never said much. I only listened."

"You like to play computer games?" he grinned at her, leaning on the table towards her, "Do your friends play them as well?"

Shifting her eyes to stare at the mirror behind him, she could feel the tears building. Her voice quiet, her bottom lip trembled, "I don't have any friends." *Dammit, I already told him I'm a loner; why does he keep asking?*

Grabbing the folder that had been sitting undisturbed on the opposite end of the table, he flipped it open, "You told your students you had a boyfriend; George. Did he like to play games with you?"

Taking in the barren eight by eight chamber, Becky blinked rapidly. The paint a dull grey, their voices echoed slightly off the walls. "Please," she whispered, fighting the deluge before it rolled down her cheeks.

Fishing a handkerchief out of a pocket, Albert Browning handed it to her. The detective was well experienced in interrogation, and familiar with the ebb and flow of the emotional state of those under scrutiny. It had been his job for over twenty years, and he was held in high regard in the art of discerning truth from fiction. "Tell me about George," he coaxed, knowing he was close to cracking her.

"I made him up," she snivelled, blowing into the cloth. "I swear, he is not a real person. I didn't want the students to see me as available, so I told them I had a boyfriend so they would leave me alone."

Pursing his lips, Albert considered the idea of creating a fake lover implausible, and her reasoning even more so. "You had issues of students harassing you in the past?" he raised an eyebrow at her.

Her mouth opening slightly, she pondered the question for a long moment. Finally, she explained as directly as she could muster; "I've never taught this age group. When we went through orientation, they made a huge deal over maintaining boundaries, and I took it to heart. I really didn't do anything wrong; I wanted to avoid anything happening. I didn't want any questions raised, and at the time, it seemed to work great."

"But you were worried about it; that's why you felt the need to lie."

"I wasn't really concerned, but everyone else, such as administration and staff, really pushed the issue. I like to think that I was being cautious," she agreed half-heartedly. "Seriously, there was nothing sinister about pretending to be involved with someone."

"Ok, so you pretended you had a significant other. Tell me how the boys in your class reacted to that; not only Jason. How did they treat you?"

Sinking back into the past, Becky sighed loudly. *They were such great kids;* at the beginning, she didn't see any of the trouble coming. Never suspected any of them were out to get her.

THREE

Keeping It Together

"Aww, COME ON, BECKY!" Alex Reyes laughed loudly, the rest of the class erupting around him.

Her face instantly bright red, "That's Miss Stewart to you!" she snapped, but the battle had already been lost. Almost from day one, the boy had picked on her, calling her by her first name and nothing she did seemed to deter it. *Why the fuck can't you act like a gentleman?* Her anger seethed below the surface, her nerves always raw.

"Come on… let's be friends," he stepped towards her, and she backed away. She knew that he wanted to hug her, which made her all the more uncomfortable.

"Go sit down!" she screamed, grabbing at drawers and searching for a referral. "Everyone, get back to your notes," she indicated the oversized digital clock. "We have eight minutes left, and then we begin the next activity."

Seeing her with the slip, Alex appeared ready to comply. Scrawling her grievances across the triplicate form, her chest heaved, and she could see the splotches on her cleavage as it rose and fell. She stared down at it, her writing paused while she gathered her wits; *son of a bitch.* She had let her anger get the better of her, and they were past the point of no return.

Holding out the sheets to him, she ignored his curses as he exited, hearing him mumbling what a bitch she was under his breath. He had gained moral support from the rest of the class over the weeks, and performed for them on his way out.

"Calm down, guys. We have work to do; we don't have time to waste on those who don't care if we get it done, either." She hated to cut ties with students, but she had to draw the line when they interfered with the learning of others. *Alex Reyes definitely interferes with the learning of others.*

They had barely started the next activity when a loud banging occurred at the door, interrupting them once more. Opening it, she stepped aside as Alex pushed his way back into her room, shoving the pink copy of the referral in her face; "He sent me back."

Snatching the sheet, Becky glared at it, feeling the warm color rising from her chest once more; *fucking great, they should have kept him.* At the bottom, she could see he had been assigned lunch detention, and they would get nothing else done that day.

Alex chose to perch on top of his desk, bouncing up and down. A pet peeve of hers, he openly goaded her.

"Please don't sit on the desk," she gritted from clenched teeth. "It breaks them and we don't have enough as it is."

Laughing, he held up his hand to accept the admiration of his peers before he plunked down into his chair. "We should call it a day, *Miss Stewart,*" he sneered, slamming the book before him closed and shoving it onto the floor as he accentuated her name.

Her fingers curled and her nails pressing into her palms, a dozen thoughts ran through her mind, and none of them had to do with the lesson. "Please pick up the book," she tried again, with every ounce of calmness she could portray.

Giving it a kick, he slid it over to another student, who bent over and retrieved the text. Placing it on his own desk, she could see the shame on the second boy's face, and she knew his plight; he wanted to learn.

But with Alex and his few cronies in class, that goal seldom came without a struggle. Glancing at the clock on the wall, she could see they were indeed short on time, and several of the students were already up, getting ready to leave.

"I haven't dismissed you yet," she snapped, which they ignored, and a few seconds later the bell rang.

Heading to lunch, the students exited the room while she glared after them, her gut wrenching in frustration. Grabbing her lunch box once the room had cleared, she headed for the department office, where she could hide for twenty five minutes, and eat before tutorials began for the second half of lunch.

Arriving in the office, she grabbed a chair and began pulling things out of her pack. Tackling the zip lock of veggies first, she crunched away as the long table filled with other adults, who conversed around her. The group seldom spoke to her, but at least they weren't rowdy kids bombarding her with senseless chatter about parties and getting drunk or high. Never having been one to use drugs, she hated listening to those heart-breaking stories the most.

Finishing off a baggy of fruit, she dug into her sandwich, and finally a cup of yogurt. Chugging her water, she gathered her trash, ready to get back to her room and change the board for her afternoon classes. Having three preps had been hard, but at least they were clumped in the schedule. She was getting the hang of setting up for the first classes in the morning, and switching everything out during lunch, and again during her conference in between the different subjects.

"We have a department meeting during the second lunch period," Glenda Pritchard reminded her crisply.

"Oh, I forgot," Becky sighed, dropping her trash into the large grey bin. "Ok, I'll be down at Gary's room in a minute. I need to put a note on my door so the kids know." She didn't have many who came to tutorials, but those that did cared about their grades, and she never wanted to let them down.

Scurrying down the hall, she entered her room in high gear. Using the eraser, she wiped almost angrily at the board, her lips moving as she silently fumed at being rushed. Opening her lesson plans to the current date, she began writing the next set, when a knock at the door interrupted her.

Stepping over, she let the group of young men enter, her smile genuine, "Hey guys; come on in. I can't stay today, but you can hang out in here if you want. If you have questions, hold them, and I'll try to get back in time to answer them."

Noting the time, she cursed under her breath; "I have to go. Stupid meetings."

Selecting a marker from the tray, Jason sidled up to her, "Want me to finish posting the lesson?"

Taken aback, she gaped at him, "You want to do that?"

"Sure," he nodded, pulling the cap off the tube. He wafted it at the box that held only a portion of the day's agenda, "It's not hard."

"Ok," she nodded, patting him on the back as she scooted behind him, "I'll be back; and thank you." Notepad in hand, she exited the room, her step picking up a slight bounce as she rushed down the hall. *He's such a good kid.* All the great ones she had made up for all the bad apples that threatened to spoil her day, and she felt grateful to have even the smallest glimmer of happiness in her otherwise dreary life.

FOUR

Mentors

"How you doin', Miss Stewart?" Bill Carver called, letting himself into the room.

Looking up from her stack of papers, Rebecca grinned and matched his drawl, "I'm doin' jus' fine!" Giggling, she indicated the mess, "I'm getting things put together so I can take them home and grade tonight; or I may save it for the weekend."

"Yeah, it's tough to juggle," he agreed, inspecting her board. "I heard you had a fight in your room the other day; thought I'd come over an' check on you."

Bill worked downtown in administration, and their typical communications happened electronically. His making an appearance in her classroom gave her an ominous feeling in her gut.

"Well, I appreciate that," she nodded slowly, shifting the stack of pages into her bag. "We got a new kid in second period; why he had to be in that class, I don't know. I guess because it's the remedial section, and that's where he belongs; along with all the rest of the hood rats, if you know what I mean. As soon as he came in, things went from bad to worse."

"That's a rough crowd," Bill agreed. "Still, you do alright with them, I think. You stand your ground, an' they need structure; otherwise they'll run over you."

"Yeah," she nodded slowly, then swallowed visibly. "I'm not in trouble or anything, am I?"

"Oh, shoot no," he chuckled loudly, taking a step back and shoving his hands into the pockets of his slacks. "I jus' wanna be here for you if you need to talk to someone. I know you're new to this type of situation, an' we all need support. How are things at home?"

Her eyes growing wide, she faltered, "At home?"

"Yeah; how's your family doing?"

Shaking her head slightly, her thoughts churned. *I don't really have any family at home;* but she couldn't tell him that. Deciding to stick with the story she had given her students, she forced a smile. "Things are good. My boyfriend, George, is taking me to a movie this weekend."

"Oh, really; which one?"

Rocking her jaw, her mind raced; *shit.* "I'm not sure. He likes to surprise me with stuff like that. You know… always the romantic type." She swiveled slightly, playing up the happy girlfriend role. *Time to go, Bill.*

Accepting her explanation, he eyed her warily and commanded, "Be sure you're taking breaks and getting out some. We're on the downhill slide to Thanksgiving, but we have a long way to go before the end of the year. You don't wanna get burned out."

"Will do," she flashed her full set of teeth and stepped towards the door, prepared to show him out. Once he had gone, she finished packing the satchel and slung it over her shoulder. Hearing the banging on her door, she sighed, and dropped the bag on the desk.

Opening the entrance, she glared at the two young women before her, "It's almost four-thirty; where have you been?"

"We had to go to math first," one of them informed her while making her way inside. "Can we still retake the test?"

"I guess so," Becky pulled out the materials and instructed them before turning them loose. She didn't like to be angry at students who were trying, but in the end, she didn't like being placed second on the list, either.

Turning to the board, she busied herself preparing for the next day while they completed the exam. Once they were done, she could send them on their way, but it was well after five pm before she climbed into her car and headed home.

Cursing the traffic, Becky longed to keep her thoughts positive. However, deep down she resented the fact that her class had not been the priority, and now she suffered as the result. Deciding to splurge on a mocha latte to lift her spirits, she turned into a shopping center and found a place to park.

Inside, she came face to face with Mark Covey, from second period, at the register, "Hey, you." *Shit;* she had forgotten that he worked there.

Becky typically avoided places where her students were employed for a number of reasons, but it was too late, and she would have to push through. Giving him her selection, she accepted the receipt and moved to the end, where a row of tall stools afforded a view of the prep area. Sliding onto one, she could watch while they made her drink and be sure that nothing happened to it.

While she glared at the process intently, the seat next to her became occupied, and she glanced over to see Jason grinning at her. His Adam's apple bobbed when he swallowed, and he spouted, "Hi," in a slight squeak.

"Hi to you, too," she wrinkled her nose slightly, noting his uniform. "I guess you work on the other side of the strip?"

"Yeah," he pointed, "Over at HH. You should come over some time; I could help you get a good deal on a new gaming system."

Hearing her name called, she nodded, "Sure; I may do that some time." Accepting her cup, she waved at both boys and headed for the door.

Back inside her car, she heaved a sigh of relief. She had never liked meeting her students in public, and after having Bill Carver in her room, it only added to her day's ups and downs. Of course, the older man was only there to help, or at least she hoped that he only wanted to help. She had been in trouble before for things that had happened in her classroom, and the thought of being on another improvement plan darkened her mood.

And what right does he have to tell me what to do on my own time? she quibbled, while staring at a red light. "He's got a wife and kids to go home to. He's in no position to judge what it's like to be me." *He's my mentor after all, but that's professional; not personal.*

Finding a place to park in the crowded lot, she sighed; *something else the lateness of those girls has cost me... my parking space.* Making the hike across to her apartment, she hauled the bag of pages needing to be graded up the stairs. Dropping it on the couch, she locked the door and hung her keys on the hook behind it.

Her eyes darting around the tiny living area, she groaned loudly. She glared at her computer, which sat on a long folding table running along the right hand wall; the focal point of the room. She wanted so badly to fire it up and become lost in a game for the rest of the evening, but the grading loomed over her.

Punching the button on the black case, she turned it on and ambled into the kitchen to put a frozen pizza in the oven.

Pulling out her chair, she stared at the bag of work with a slight pout on her lip.

Opting to play for a bit while she ate, she promised herself she would get onto the homework as soon as she had finished. She placed her headset over her ears and opened up Ventrilo so she could talk to her friends. Keying the mic, "Hey, fellas. What's going on tonight?" she grinned with anticipation.

Instantly greeted by a dozen voices, calling to her from around the world, she sighed. *See? I do have friends.* The fact that she had never met any of them in person shouldn't matter. *They still care about me.* "What're we doing tonight?" she asked again, having not gotten a clear response.

"We're setting up a raid right now," TeeTops informed her, "And you're healing, so get on your mage and let's roll, HotStuff!"

Becky giggled at the nickname of one of her characters, having chosen it for just that reason. "Sure thing, Tee; let me get situated, and I'll be right there." Pushing back her chair, she moved to retrieve her pizza and grab another drink. *Forget the grading; I can always do it this weekend.* A few minutes later, she had become lost in the pixels and the violence of electronic murder, casting all thoughts of her mundane life at Central High aside.

FIVE

Day In, Day Out

"DID you end up on an improvement plan?" Detective Browning tapped the end of his pen against his notepad in front of him.

"No, not that time," she frowned, shifting in her chair. "Any chance I could get something to drink? You guys have had me in here for hours."

"Sure," he closed his folder and stood, "You want coffee or water?"

"Coffee, please."

"I can send someone to escort you to the bathroom if you like," he played nice for the moment.

"Yes," she made it to her feet stiffly, "That's a good idea." Studying him, she managed a small smile, and an even larger one for the female officer who appeared over his shoulder.

Arriving in the next hallway, Al could hear the increased level of noise coming from the lobby of the precinct. Catching a patrol officer passing by, he wafted a hand towards the ruckus, "What's going on out there?"

"Oh, the media got wind of the interrogation, so they're

packed into the front; all waiting for the scoop," the younger man replied.

"Well, that's great," Browning muttered, continuing down the hall. Stopping in an open office, he called loudly, "We got any bloodwork back yet?"

"No," his partner, Andrew Martin, dropped a folder on his desk, "But the coroner sent photos of the Reyes autopsy. They aren't pretty. How's it going in there?"

"Well, I didn't figure they would be," he lifted the file and peeked at the stack of pictures. "She has trust issues, and is sticking to her story. We're on the third run through, and it don't vary much. She's getting tired though, so if she's going to crack, I'm thinking it'll be soon."

"Yeah; you'll want to look over some of these interviews when you have time," Detective Martin shook his notebook at him. "They all say basically the same thing. Let me know when you're ready to change it up; maybe we could tag out."

"Will do," Al slapped the other man on the arm, and headed on to locate a cup of java for his perp.

Left alone after her welcome trip to the bathroom, Rebecca picked at her nails, her thoughts continuing on from her late night of gaming and the hell that it cost her the following day. Exhausted from the raid that had only ended when she insisted that she had to get to bed, she had gone in to work on only three hours of sleep.

Of course, being tired had only added to her issues with her trouble students, and she had found herself yelling at one of them how stupid it was to get a referral on a Friday; it's an easy day and why couldn't he just sit down and shut up already. She was still kicking herself over that one.

When Browning returned, she accepted the warm cup of brew and looked up at the officer with doleful eyes, "Can I get another smoke as well?"

Pulling out the pack, he placed it before her. Staring at her rounded belly, he knew she risked damaging her infant, but in the end, that was her choice to make. "Let's see," he recapped instead, "You made it to Thanksgiving break, and things seemed to be going pretty well."

"Yeah," she agreed, flicking the lighter and taking a long drag. "Yeah, things went good... well, they went ok. We still had the problems with those guys wanting to kick each other's asses all the time. And I started having things in my classroom destroyed and vandalized."

"Did you suspect Alex Reyes and those thugs in the morning of doing it? Or was it one of the students from the afternoon?"

"I have no idea; I never caught anyone. I would find the stuff broken later, which really hurt my feelings. I provided all that stuff that we used; I pay for it myself, so when they tear it up, it comes out of my pocket to replace it."

"That added to your stress level," he read the lines in her face.

"Yup; but I had my good classes, too." Staring at her half-empty cup, she sighed, "When fourth period finished their work, they would sit around and talk; I found that pretty relaxing. And all those guys were gamers, so we would get into classes, and archetypes; gaming stuff. Plus, they were up on what was coming out new. I liked that they kept me in the loop."

"Did any of them know where you played? I mean, did they look you up and join you online?"

"No," she shook her head profusely. "I never gave them my screen name, or my servers. I told you, I was a professional in my classroom, and avoided anything that could lead to trouble or contact off campus as well."

"And things went from there."

"Yeah," she agreed, turning an open palm to the ceiling, "Day in, day out. They came to class and did their work, and all my classes moved along as fast and as far as I could push them."

Pulling out his pad, Browning made a few notes, his mind briefly flashing to the crowd that had gathered out front. She had called herself a professional, and if her story rang true, he had to admit she hadn't done anything that could be considered illegal. Of course, he doubted if the press, or the public for that matter, would see it that way.

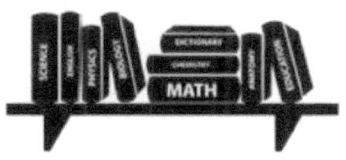

SIX

Empty Walls

"HEY, Miss Stewart; whatcha gonna be doing for the holiday?" Jason called in a friendly voice from across the room.

"As little as possible," she laughed, putting him off without giving him any details about her private life. Stopping, she picked up a pair of broken scissors and sighed; *damn.* "Why do kids do this shit?" she held up the objects, her face instantly turning bright red when she heard herself curse. During second lunch, only the two of them occupied her room; *it's still no reason to use that kind of language.*

Laughing at her, he shook his head and resumed his writing on her white board, "Because they're assholes, miss."

"Hey, I didn't mean to cuss, and you can't either," she cut her eyes over at him and tossed the bits in the trash.

"It's ok." he shifted his gaze to meet hers, "You need to lighten up. You're a young woman; you don't need to get all down, like the old salty bitches around here."

Rolling her eyes, she tried to stay calm, "Really, Jason; I wish you wouldn't use that kind of language."

Laughing at her, he adjusted his grip on the marker and

went on with his posting, "Whatever, miss. You act like grownups don't use bad words."

"Well, they do," she admitted, "Let me slide behind you," she offered, making her way to her desk while her hand brushed against his back. The touch ever so slight, it gave her an odd feeling in the pit of her stomach; *don't touch the students.*

Adjusting into her chair, she giggled as she recalled the warning they had been given over and over during their summer training; *at least a hundred times, in fact.* Of course, she never did if she could help it, but in the cramped space, contact was inevitable. "I really appreciate you taking over the posting every day; it really helps."

"Yes, ma'am," he turned to face her, standing over her as she flipped through the tabs on her monitor to locate her email. "Anyways, I hope you have a good Christmas break." He placed his hand on the back of her chair and leaned over her slightly, his proximity adding to her discomfort.

Considering how to tactfully remove him from her space, she heard a knock on the door. "Could you get that for me? I need to get everything cleared up so I can leave at the bell this afternoon."

Letting a few of the other students in, he returned to her, this time taking a position across, on the other side of her desk. "I wish you'd just tell me what you're going to be doing. It's not like I'm stalking you or anything," he chuckled loudly when he said it.

Her eyes darting to meet his, she could see the playful look in them; "You know, we're not friends, Jason. I like you; but you're my student. I'm not at liberty to discuss whatever plans my *boyfriend* and I have for the holiday." She exaggerated the word boyfriend, hoping he would back off and stop giving her the creepy vibe she sometimes picked up from him.

Hearing another knock, he sneered, "Yeah, right, miss."

His expression startled her, and she wondered for a moment if he knew she was lying to him. The bell chimed before she could respond, and Becky stood to take over at the door, calling loudly, "You guys get out your books and notes. We're going to finish off the last chapter before the holiday break."

Ignoring their groans, she pushed against the wide wooden covering and stood in the hall, but peeked back into the room often to monitor the students and ensure they were doing as they were asked. This had become her best class, and although it remained the largest, she could count on them to be the high point of her day.

Arriving home a few hours later, she slammed the door shut enthusiastically, and locked it behind her. Placing her keys on the hook, she darted across to the computer and fired it up. Skipping to the tiny bedroom, she dug through her pile of laundry to locate a clean pair of pajamas and quickly slipped them on. "Double XP; double XP," she sang aloud.

The event had started earlier that day, and she couldn't wait to get logged in and see where everyone had congregated. With the bonus experience points, the guild would be hopping, and she should have a pretty good selection of groups to join. "Hey, guys, guess who's here!" she called into her mic after she plunked into her chair.

"Hey, hey, Teach!" a male voice replied affectionately.

"Hey, Broncho; where's the party?"

"Saddle up, missy, we're meeting up for some PVP," he informed her, "We need tanks and DPS at this point."

"Ok, let me get logged in, and I'll see what I can bring," she stuffed her mouth with a huge bite of sandwich and washed it down with a swig of soda. *It's my fucking holiday, I'll spend it however I want.* She had talked to her mother on the way to the apartment, and still felt a little angry that the older woman had tried to guilt her into coming home for Christmas.

That's easy for her to say, though. She's not the one who has to drive ten fucking hours to make that happen. Choosing a beefy looking character from her wide selection, she keyed the mic, "Ok, I'm bringing Smasher; that's my tank. I'll be right there."

Becoming lost in her game and online friends, her computer had become like a drug; an addiction that seemed to push out every other part of her life. Recalling the conversation she had shared with Jason earlier, she briefly wondered what he and the rest of her students would be doing over the holiday. *Of course, they still live at home, so keeping their mommas happy is easy for them.*

At thirty years old, Becky had given up on keeping her mother happy long ago. The woman had become obsessed with fixing her daughter up with men every time she visited, and every phone call at some point led to a discussion about grandchildren. *Why can't she just leave me alone?*

By the age of twenty five, the young teacher had sworn to herself that she would never get trapped in that scenario. Giving up her time and energy on raising a child wasn't for her, and she knew it. Besides, she liked her little apartment with her empty walls and bachelor-esque lifestyle. Deep down, she could admit to herself that having to share her space full time was not worth fixing the momentary bouts of loneliness she occasionally faced. *I don't need that shit, plain and simple.*

Focusing on her game, she pushed the dark thoughts aside. This was her holiday, and she had earned it, as much if not more than anyone else. *And anyone who says any different can kiss my ass.*

SEVEN

Looking Up

"WELL, FUCK." Becky cursed, dabbing makeup under her eyes. She had spent the last two weeks immersed in raids, questing, and player on player combat, and her features clearly reflected her lack of sleep. "But… it was worth it," she added with a grin.

The long break had done her good, as far as she was concerned, and they were on the downhill side of the year. Things were looking up, and she refused to wallow in the dark thoughts that would ultimately bring her down.

Making her way to her classroom, she had made it to the school early, feeling eager to get on with the day. Inside, she set up the audio-visual equipment that had been stored for the break and laid out the supplies they would need for the day's lesson. While she worked, she hummed quietly to herself, until she heard her door open. Turning to see who had entered, a surprised expression crossed her face when her department chair, Gary Burdette stood before her.

"Good morning, Rebecca," he greeted warmly.

"Hiya, Gary," she smiled back, only pausing for a moment,

then continuing with her prepping. "What can I do for you?" she could feel her heart rate climbing.

"Oh, I don't know," he hemmed and hawed, his hand trailing lightly along the edge of a student desk, "It seems you've had an ok year so far, and I'm hoping that is going to continue."

Stopping, the young woman pivoted to face him, "And?"

"Well, we've had some complaints right at the end of the semester, and I gave myself the holiday to decide what to do about them."

Shit; I'm in fucking trouble... again. "Listen, Gary; whatever this is about, I'm sure it's unfounded," she dug right in, not waiting to hear the details of the situation.

"I hope that it is," he nodded a few times, "But we have to act, none the less."

Frowning heavily, she turned her back on him. *Fucking great;* "Ok, what is it, then?"

"Some of your female students say that you play favorites; that you're more lenient on the boys, and give them higher grades," he blurted. "I'm sure it's not intentional, and I went through your semester averages to get a feel for the situation. I hate to say that it does appear that there's some form of favoritism going on there; maybe that you're not even aware of..." his voice faded.

"No way!" she exclaimed, her face shooting up and eyes glaring at him. "I would never!"

"Not on purpose, but the evidence speaks for itself," he soothed.

"There has to be some other explanation," she breathed, "I treat them all the same!"

"I'm sorry, Becky. I'm going to give you until the progress reports go out at the three week mark to self-evaluate. I'll run your numbers then, and if things have improved, we'll leave it at this level."

"And if they haven't improved? I'm telling you, if the boys are doing better, it's because they work harder!" her voice rose in her rebuttal.

"I doubt that," he chuckled, shaking his head. "But, you're aware of it now, so keep an eye on what you're doing. Maybe it's when you're grading, or during the class. Maybe you're interacting differently between the boys and the girls, and that's giving them some sort of an advantage."

"Yeah, right," she sneered, turning her back on him and squeezing her fingers into fists. "Thanks, Gary. I'll figure it out," she dismissed him. Sinking into her chair after he had left the room, she placed her elbows on her desk and pushed her face into her hands; *why is this happening to me?*

Every year it had been something different. This year, she had those assholes in her morning classes that picked on her and made things so difficult. *What about them?* But that's how administration works; *always fixing the teachers instead of the students, and never taking what we say seriously.* No wonder so many teachers quit.

She had been complaining for months about the group in her morning class that called her by her first name. The ones that openly disrespected her and the rest of the students; not to mention all the destruction that took place between the supplies, the desks, and the textbooks. *But that's my fault as well, because I don't watch them closely enough.* She knew if the can of worms were opened with her grading, it wouldn't stop there.

Her mood spoiled, she finished putting everything out, slamming cabinets and drawers while she was at it.

"Wow, you're in a good mood!"

Hearing the male voice behind her, Becky spun around, "How'd you get in here?" she breathed.

"The door's unlocked," Jason grinned, indicating the entrance with an extended appendage. "I came by to see how your holiday was, but from the looks of it; not good."

"God dammit," she fumed, "I hate it when they come into my room and leave the doors open."

"You're the only teacher I know who keeps it that way," he chided gently.

Fumbling with her keys, she moved to rectify the situation, sputtering, "They're supposed to. It's a security risk having all the doors unlocked; and it's against policy. People only come into my room when I let them in," *or they have a key,* she silently added bitterly.

"What… do you think someone is out to get you?" his voice sounded condescending.

"No," she laughed him off, twisting the handle to test it, "I don't think people are out to get me," but deep down she felt the jolt of fear. The truth was, she often felt afraid that her class would one day be splattered across the front page news after an act of violence. *It's only a matter of time, with the students I often have on my roster.* "It's just not right to have it where anyone who wants can come barging in, Jason; just leave it at that."

"Ah," he raised his chin at her, then gave her a warm smile, "So, how was your Christmas break?"

"It was fine," she returned to her work, then paused. "Are you visiting all your teachers, or should I feel special?" she asked cautiously.

"I planned to visit a few," he dropped his books on a desk, "We'll see how far I make it." Lifting her lesson plan book, he flipped to the right page and began to put the morning's agenda on the board. "Mine was great, by the way, thank you for asking."

"Sorry; call me anti-social," she grinned at his cheekiness,

"Glad to hear it, though." She observed him more calmly, "You don't have to do that."

"Naw, I like to help," he cut his dark brown eyes over at her, curling his lips in a way that made her stomach flop.

He's a student, she reminded herself, and turned her back on him to finish shifting the desks for the first activity. *What if this is the 'special treatment' the girls think the boys are getting?* The thought horrified her, and she covertly stole glances at him while his hand glided across the shiny white surface; *oh, God.* How long had he been coming to her room and helping her outside of class?

Finished with the task, Jason clapped the notebook closed with a flourish, "It is done, my lady."

"Thanks," she accepted the binder and put it in its place, with the rest of her resources. Pausing, she felt guilty at what she would say next and hoped he took it well; "I really appreciate your help, Jason. But, I think I should put the lessons on the board myself from now on."

"Why?" His face instantly grew dark, standing only inches from her, "Am I not doing it right?"

"You're doing it fine," she clenched her fist to prevent her hand from landing on his arm, and her bottom lip began to quiver.

Picking up on her distress, he reached out to her, "What's wrong, miss?"

Pulling away at the brush of his fingers on her cheek, she stared up at him, 'I appreciate your help, but I don't think you coming in here alone and helping me is a good thing. I think it needs to stop."

Taking a step back, she refused to give him anything further. Instead, she wiped her hands down the front of her pants, as if she were removing some distasteful smudge from them. "You better go, hun. See how those other teachers' holidays went."

Placing the expo marker he'd been toying with in the tray, he could hear the sadness in her voice. Blinking for a moment, he gave her a sideways glare and gathered his things, "You sure are acting weird."

"It's ok," she sniffled, "I have to work this out for myself. You go on, and I'll see you in class." The room felt barren after he left, and it occurred to her that the number of people who did nice things for her were few in number. *The people who make me feel appreciated; damn.*

Glancing around at the empty desks, she knew that they soon would be filled with talking, laughing, living youth. *They hate me,* she muttered to herself. Most of her students wouldn't lift a finger for her, and she briefly allowed her mind to wonder. *If a student, or anyone for that matter, were to come barging in with a gun... or a knife, even!*

Yeah, if someone were stabbing me to death, these guys wouldn't do a thing to stop them. Reaching for her Kleenex, she dabbed at her tears and wiped the snot that had begun to drip as she wallowed in her sorrow. *They wouldn't help; they would whip out their phones and start filming it... or chanting and urging them on.* On her way in this morning, she had thought her year was looking up; *so much for that.*

EIGHT

Innocence Lost

"So, you think your students were out to get you?" Detective Browning demanded in a condescending tone.

Surprised, Rebecca's jaw dropped, and she stared at him with wide eyes. "No," she clipped. "Not in so many words. Not at that point."

"Well, good," he shifted anxiously and smoothed his hair, "Because at this point, all you've got are a few broken pairs of scissors and a couple of marked up text books."

Blinking rapidly, her mind raced, "Yeah, it started out slow; like whoever was doing it was just getting warmed up." She shuddered, knowing how bad things were going to get. "Anyways, Jason did as I asked, more or less."

"He stopped coming to your room and helping?"

"No, he stopped coming alone," she admitted quietly. "He always brought a friend or two after that. And that's when I really started to feel all weird about him."

"You were attracted to him?"

"No," she giggled nervously, rubbing the top of her rounded belly, "Not like that. I mean, come on! He's a student, for one.

And he was twelve years younger than me, for another. It was creepy and my skin crawled at the very idea of it; I had never even thought about students in that way and wasn't about to start."

"Then why did it make you feel strange?" Albert's voice dropped, drawing on her emotions.

"Because…" she swallowed hard, "He started doing things. Little things." She paused, then her voice suddenly grew loud, "You know, everyone thinks that kids are all sweet and innocent; but they're not. They're like little adults, with their own agenda. They want things, and they know how to get them. Like those little bastards that were in my second period."

"The ones that you filed the grievance against."

"Yes, them! They had been picking at me since day one. Only they had been playing the system for a long time. Take Alex Reyes; he knew where the line was, and he stayed right on the edge of it. He would disrupt class and push my buttons, but never in a way that would actually get him in trouble. He was a heckler, and the only thing he wanted was to ruin it for everyone else. And the other kids hated his disruptions as much as I did… at least the ones that weren't joining him, that is."

"What does that have to do with Jason?"

Her eyes grew misty, the thought of her favorite student's manipulation painful. "He was nice to me," she drew a ragged breath, "But it wasn't because he liked me. It was a game to him, only I couldn't see it." A tear escaped, and she brushed it away. "He started making off-color comments; even in class, he would insinuate things, like something was going on between us."

"And how did you handle this?"

"Well, I had two choices, really. I could get all bent out of shape and escalate the situation, or I could let it go. I chose to laugh it off, as in good fun, but nothing serious," she wrung the handkerchief he had handed her earlier, "Sometimes I would even play along. It was funny, in a way, like everyone was in on the joke, and we laughed about it. Like I was actually a part of their group. We joked about it, and it didn't mean anything."

"You liked the attention."

"Yeah," she stared at his tie, not looking him in the eye. "I liked feeling that someone liked me. Like some of my kids didn't want to get me fired, and actually appreciated all the time and effort I put into teaching them."

"So then what happened?"

"Well, time passed, and things really did seem to be getting better. My grades checked out at the three week point, and that took some of the stress off of me." She paused, not daring to admit how she had spent a few hours making sure to raise all of the girls' grades a few points each to ensure it would happen.

"Anyway, things rolled along, until the week before spring break; that's when they got ugly in a hurry," she sighed loudly.

"Yes, this is where the grievance came from."

"Yeah, I know those boys did it. I was ninety-nine percent sure of it."

Exhaling loudly, Browning shifted in his chair and opened the file. "Ok, walk me through all of this, starting with the first incident, and we'll take it from there."

"The first thing that happened was the bloody maxi pad. Only, it wasn't really blood. It was hot sauce, or something I found it inside my purse when I reached for my keys at the end of the day."

"Your purse wasn't locked up?" he demanded doubtfully.

"Yes, it was, but I later found out that the cheap little locks on all our drawers and cabinets were easy to bypass if you knew how; that's how I knew it had to be Alex and the hoodlums in second. Same with our doors, for that matter. I found out anyone with a knife or a credit card could open them in a few seconds," she defended.

"You didn't report this incident, though."

"No, not at the time. I was mortified to find it there, so I threw it away, and did nothing," she pouted slightly, realizing that had not been entirely true. After that, she began watching certain students more closely, hoping to catch them in the act of something concrete. "And the next thing that happened I couldn't prove either."

"The poisoning."

"Right. I accidentally left my water bottle out, and I knew immediately that it tasted funny; I shouldn't have finished it. But sadly, I did, and then I got violently ill afterwards," her features drooped. "It had happened to me a few years ago, at the ninth grade school. A student put eye drops in my coffee, but another student reported them. That's how I knew what this was; it felt exactly the same."

"I see," he scribbled on his yellow pad for a moment, "Then what?"

"Then I started finding the condoms; a few at first, and then a crap ton all at once. They appeared to have been used, and tied shut," she rubbed her fingers against her palms, feeling dirty. "That's when I called Gary in, and tried to file a complaint."

"Where were these condoms?"

"Oh my God, they were everywhere!" she exclaimed. "Inside of drawers; inside of cabinets. There was a book on the counter that one of the girls picked up and it fell open to one; she started screaming like it were a snake or something!"

"Wow, I bet that was disruptive."

"Sure as hell was," she growled, "We didn't get anything done after that."

"What did your department chair do?"

"He made notes, and gave me a pair of gloves to dispose of them all. I spent an entire Saturday going through every inch of the room, removing and throwing them away; and cleaning," she scowled at the loss of her personal day taking care of a student's bad behavior.

"How many were there?"

"Fifty two," she replied crisply. "I counted them, and I was so angry. I really came down on them after that, trying to find out who did it for real."

"Whoa, that's a lot of condoms. Actually, I don't think this is just one kid doing all this," his face wrinkled as he spoke.

"No," she sat up straighter, stabbing the table before her, "And I didn't think so either. That's how I knew it had to be a conspiracy. Those guys had to be working together, and I was determined to prove it."

"I don't see that there was an actual police report or anything like that made at the time, though," he countered gently. "Are you sure of the dates on this?"

"Absolutely," she nodded her head vigorously, "It was the week before spring break; that Friday in fact. I had to give up the first day of my vacation to rectify it, and then Gary didn't even file a report for me."

"And how did that make you feel?"

"Well, as if I had been cheated, of course!" her voice grew loud, "Not only were the kids out to get me, administration didn't have my back. It was like I could suddenly see things for how they really were. No one cared about me, or my efforts, and no one was going to help me," she grew quiet. "That's when I came up with my plan."

"You decided to get even with the kids."

Staring at the table once more, Becky rubbed at her chin anxiously. "No one was supposed to get hurt," she breathed quietly. "I just wanted to teach them a lesson. Something small and simple, that would get their attention."

Albert tapped the table with the end of his pen, waiting for her to continue. He knew where this was going, and hoped this time she would give up the details he needed to put this case to rest.

NINE

Song and Dance

GOD DAMMIT! Becky swore under her breath as she slammed the door to her car. Switching on the engine, she threw the vehicle into reverse and backed out of her assigned spot, glaring at her mutilated antenna. At least this time, they had made an actual report. *I bet it's only because I went to campus security instead of to Gary,* she fumed.

It had been three weeks since spring break, and something new happened every day, it seemed like. Her desks were broken, with screws being removed from underneath and the brackets left hanging. Textbooks were missing pages, or having penises drawn inside them. She strongly suspected someone was removing the books in their backpacks to make the alterations, and returning them later, so they couldn't be caught.

Son of a bitch! she slapped at the steering wheel, her anger gushing over in the form of salty tears. *Why do they hate me so badly?* Her mind spinning, her shoulders began to shake violently as she sobbed. *I'm so sick of this song and dance; trying to be nice to people who are so fucking mean to me.* She had formulated her plan for revenge after nothing had been done about the condoms, but had been too timid to carry it out.

Mother fuckers, she bit angrily, turning into the parking lot of a local grocery store. Damaging her car had been the last straw. *This is going to end, one way or another.* Climbing out, she slammed the car door and stomped inside. Wiping at her tear stained cheeks, she grabbed a basket and headed to the pharmacy, where she selected a few boxes of chocolate flavored ex-lax.

Spinning around, she marched straight to the aisle lined with boxes of baked goods. Pouring over the selection of cakes and pies, she started to choose brownies, but decided that cupcakes would be easier to control. *After all, I don't want to make everyone sick.* Picking up a few of the foil pans and a couple of canisters of brightly colored frosting, she headed to the front.

An hour later, her oven beeped loudly, indicating that it was ready to go. Placing the first pan inside, she squatted down in front of the device to watch them bake. When the buzzer went off, she gingerly lifted them out and placed them on the counter to cool. *I sure as hell hope this works.*

She had found the recipe ages ago; *cupcakes with a bite of chocolate hidden inside.* This batch held plain old bits of Hershey bar; *this is the test.* If it worked, her students would eat them up, and those with the special version would later get a nasty surprise. Grabbing one, she couldn't wait any longer, and crushed it, breaking it open.

"Holy shit!" she squealed aloud, "It's perfect!" The chocolate goo strung out as she pulled the two halves apart, and she popped one of them into her mouth, feeling instant joy at her success.

It took her half the night to complete the process, and she carefully marked the plates that would go to the group she intended to punish. Everyone else would get a regular treat, and none would be the wiser. She giggled to herself at how easy it was going to be, since she had gerrymandered the groups after they came back from spring break.

Normally, groups were arranged so that each one had a high level student, two mediums, and a low. That way, they could work together, and help lift each other up. "Not any more, though," she cackled out loud.

After spring break, she had placed all of the low end in second period in one group; *the loser's table.* She'd been fed up with them, and now they would get what they deserved. Of course, the students were happy; they didn't get how the groups were arranged to begin with, or why. Being allowed to sit with their friends felt like a victory to them. *Oh, little do they know.*

Placing the plates into boxes to carry, Becky hummed to herself. Her preparation complete, she carried out the trash before she bounced off to bed, but found herself unable to sleep. Going over the dispensing of her special surprise over and over, her excitement grew.

The following morning, she made several trips to get all of the boxes into her car. Being sure to get there earlier than normal, she made her way inside, hoping to keep her special day between her and her students. *We're not supposed to give the kids food,* she recalled. *It's against some federal rule, so the school can get fined; but fuck 'em.* At that moment, she felt above the law and didn't really care if it upset anyone.

Stacking the boxes into a cabinet, she locked the doors afterwards, having taken great care to line them up properly. When she pulled them out for each class, she knew that the marked plates would land on the loser's table, and justice would be served.

Noting her bright smile when Jason knocked on her door and entered with a few of his friends, he observed, "Wow, you're in a good mood today."

"Oh, yes, sweetheart; I am. I'm doing a special lesson with the morning classes," she teased.

"Haha; that's cool," he grabbed the notebook and selected a marker. "You doing anything fun this weekend?"

"I have a big raid planned, actually," she admitted, while shuffling through pages and missing the glance he shared with one of the other boys. "You know I don't like to share too much about my personal life with you guys," she finished, taking a seat in front of her computer.

"Yeah, we know," the other boy laughed. "But it's not a big deal, Miss Stewart."

"Well, it is to me," she countered evenly, immersing herself in her email and ignoring their friendly banter. A few minutes later the trio left, and she moved to the hall, holding her door open. Bouncing slightly, she couldn't wait for the day to begin.

TEN

Retribution

"COME ON GUYS, get in your chairs!" Miss Stewart called loudly, trying to keep herself together. "We have a great lesson planned for today, and we need to be on task!"

Reluctantly taking their seats, the loser's table continued to laugh and talk loudly, so she began to pass out their treats, starting on the far side of the room. "Brandy, would you mind giving everyone a cup and a napkin, and Mark can pour the lemonade," she directed calmly.

Seeing that she was handing out food, Alex called out excitedly, "You're feeding us, miss?"

"Yeah, we're going to do a little writing assignment to go along with this," she grinned deviously, "So sit still and let me get everyone situated." Carefully working her way across, she made sure the special batch landed on their table. "There you go guys; each of you gets two."

"Wow, thanks, miss!" Alex's eyes grew wide as he tore into the first one.

One of the other boys at his table gave the treat a dubious glare, before announcing, "I'm allergic to chocolate."

"That's ok, I got you covered," Kevin Marquez grabbed the extra pair and put them on his napkin.

"No, wait!" she reached out, then caught herself before she protested too loudly; *fuck!* She hadn't thought of that, but knew she couldn't make too big of a deal, or she might get caught. "It's really not fair if you eat extra," she covered more quietly.

"It's ok, miss. Jesus, you make a big deal about everything!" one of the other students belittled her, and she suddenly wished she had fed the whole class laxatives.

"I see," she drew a calming breath, and reached for her back up plate. "I did make a few extras, so if anyone needs another, here you go." Turning her back on them, she faced the door and grinned broadly before screwing her face back into a more normal countenance. "You have about five minutes, and then we will need to get on to the important part of the lesson."

"Yeah, cause the important part is never the fun part," someone shouted from behind her.

"It's the fun part for me," Becky countered, locating her stack of paper and distributing the supplies. "Alex, do you wanna carry around the trash can so everyone can toss their cups and napkins?"

Staring at her in surprise, he laughed, "What, do I look like your slave? That's racist, miss."

Chuckling at the image of him in a few hours, she replied, "It's not racist; ninety percent of my students are not white, so how about you help out for once, and stop being an ass about it."

"I'll do it, miss," another boy got to his feet and manned the oversized receptacle.

"Thanks," she muttered, her eyes still locked with the young man who made her life hell on a daily basis; *don't worry, son... things are about to be squared.*

Becky was seated in the tiny office, scarfing her lunch,

when she got the first inkling that something had gone wrong. Glenda Pritchard entered the room, huffing loudly and pointing a pudgy finger at her; "They're looking for you."

"For me? Why?"

"One of your kids is sick, and he says you fed them cupcakes today."

Her hands shaking, Rebecca shoved her remaining items back into her lunch bag. "We did a little project today. It wasn't any big deal."

"You're not supposed to give the students food," Anna informed her crisply, tossing her blond locks, "It's against the rules."

"I know, and it was only this once," she grabbed her pack and headed out the door, suddenly grateful she had carried out the trash from her apartment when she finished last night. *If it goes that far, at least they won't have any proof that I spiked the cakes.*

Arriving at her classroom, she found Gary and the campus security guard poking around inside. "These all look the same," the officer pointed out, his glove covered hands lifting the large paper serving plates out of the trash.

"Of course they're the same," she clipped, interrupting them. "It was a tactile exercise to go with a writing assignment, and all of the students did it. What's wrong with that?" she feigned innocence.

"A couple of the kids have gotten ill," Gary supplied, "Where did you get these?"

"I baked them," she covered her racing heart with her right hand, her bosom rising and falling in an exaggerated manner, "Are they ok?" Real concern crept up her spine; *oh, shit! What if one of them were really allergic?*

"They will be; we're just trying to ascertain the cause of their illness. As it stands, it's six kids, with diarrhea and vomiting. They think you poisoned them," the officer noted the smile that flittered across her face as he spoke.

"Most certainly not," she denied, quickly replacing the tiny grin with an expression of pure shock, "I would never do such a thing!" *Guilty conscience, perhaps?* she tacked on telepathically, confident she had gotten the parties who had been harassing her. "I hope that they find the real cause of this."

Placing all of the plates into a clean trash bag, the officer didn't say anything else before he left the room. Watching him take the evidence, Becky fidgeted with the hem of her blouse. "I'm sorry, Gary," she muttered. "I never expected anyone to get sick. I was trying to come up with something they would enjoy; so they would like my class better," she lied flatly.

"I know," he reached over, giving her a firm pat on the shoulder, "And I appreciate your efforts. However, any more special lessons will need to be cleared by me beforehand, you got that?"

"Am I in trouble?" she blinked at him, her eyes filling with tears.

"Not yet," he shook his head, moving towards the door, "But you're working on it," he tossed over his shoulder as he exited the room.

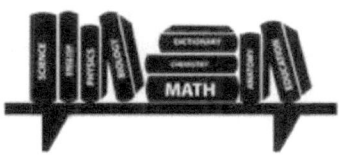

ELEVEN

Guilty as Charged

"YOU GOTTA BE KIDDING ME!" Becky slammed her fist down on the table, her eyes darting around the ring of faces staring at her "After all this time, and all my complaints, NOW you wanna do something?"

"Calm down, ma'am," the principal adjusted his tie, "There's no reason to become overly emotional."

"No reason?" her voice shook, then bellowed, "NO REASON? From the first month of school I have complained about those boys. I have written referrals; I have called parents, and had no less than THREE conferences scheduled, none of which took place because the PARENTS didn't show up!"

"They have disrupted my class. They have destroyed my classroom; and not just the stuff that I bought. Books and desks have also been damaged," she pushed on. "They are the ones at fault here!"

"You have no proof that any of those boys are responsible for any of those things," the campus officer pointed out. "They are effectively empty accusations."

"Oh yeah?" she sneered, "What proof do you have that I poisoned them? Huh?" her eyes flicked from person to person.

"You don't! Only now, because it's them accusing ME, I'm in trouble."

"It's the mere fact that it's the same boys you have had trouble with that makes you appear guilty," Gary folded his hands in front of him, leaning on them with his chin. "Please, Becky; be reasonable. You aren't being punished."

"I am!" she screamed. "I'm the one being placed on an improvement plan, here. And you don't have a shred of proof; other than I fed them cupcakes. And I have told you that they are messing with me! Who says they are really sick? How do you know they're not claiming to be as another way to get at me?"

"Kevin Marquez earned a trip to the hospital; I doubt that he's faking it," the principal countered.

"Well, how do you know he didn't eat the shit on his own? They're all friends, maybe they did something before school, and this is their way of shifting the blame to someone else; me!"

The entire group glared at her. Wiggling uneasily, Gary tried to smooth things over. "Miss Stewart, we all want this to work out. We want you to finish out the year, and for your students to do well in your class. We also have parents to contend with."

"Oh, the parents are all upset, aren't they?" she growled, "Before, they couldn't be bothered to come and see me."

Tapping his pen noisily against the conference room table, Principal Hayes cleared his throat. "I think this has gone far enough. You will sign the plan, and you will stick to it. Otherwise," he slid a bright yellow notepad across the table towards her, "You can write out your resignation and we'll walk you to your car." Getting to his feet, he left the room, the remainder of the group sitting in stunned silence.

Picking up the stack of pages, Becky began to shuffle through them, tears spilling over and running down her face;

damn them. Damn them all. But it's only three weeks until the end. *Surely I can make it to the end.* "Will this plan be in effect next year?" she asked quietly.

Exchanging glances with the others, Gary shrugged, "I don't see that it would be. We want to help you finish out the year, and keep everybody happy."

"So this is purely CYA. You guys covering your asses, once again."

Extending his index fingers, he tapped them lightly against his lips before he replied, "We do want everyone to be happy, and protected. Call it what you will, but this is how it is. Sign the paper, and return to your class. Hang on for three more weeks, and you get another chance next year, with a fresh group of kids."

Sighing loudly, Becky uncapped the pen. Glaring at the line, she ground her teeth for a moment before angrily scrawling her name across it. "Fine." Shoving the papers to the center of the table, she pushed back her chair and stormed out of the room.

In her class, one of the grade level principals stood at the front, watching as the group of students read silently from their textbooks. When she entered, everyone looked up, and voices began to whisper from one side of the room to the other. "Pipe down, everyone," she commanded. "Please, finish up with your notes. We have work to do."

Not speaking to the man at the head of her class, she grabbed a stack of assignments and began handing them out. "I've graded these reports. Most of them are excellent work. Those of you who didn't score at least a seventy may redo them to improve your grade; as per district policy," she clipped, noting when the visitor left them.

As soon as he was gone, the class erupted, with students out of their seats and moving around. She felt pulled in several directions at once by those who clamored for an explanation.

"What happened?" Jason demanded louder than anyone. Grabbing her arm, he forced her to face him, pure concern woven across his brow.

"It's nothing," she lied flatly, catching his hand and removing it from her appendage. "Seriously, get back to your work. We don't have time to waste on stupid sh… stuff," she caught herself before she cursed.

Unmoved, Jason stepped towards her, and she held up her hands to ward him off. He refused to be detoured, and folded his arms around her, pulling her against him. "It's ok, miss," his stroked her hair. "We all believe in you."

The closest she had ever let him get to her, his scent encouraged her to relax against him and breath him in. Sobbing loudly, she clung to his pressed plaid shirt, accepting his comfort.

Several other students reached out to pat her on the arms, shoulders and back, pushing her over the edge; *they do care about me!* In the midst of the most horrible day she could remember, her students were there for her.

Dabbing at her tears, she extricated herself and smiled up at him, "You guys know you're my best class. No matter how bad my day is, I know I can count on you."

Clinging to a few of her fingers, Jason still appeared distraught, while the rest of the students slowly shifted back into their seats to continue the lesson. Patting her on the back, he grinned down at her, their eyes locked for a moment before he let her go and sank back into his chair, returning to his text.

TWELVE

Graduation

Oh, my God I made it! Becky squealed to herself as she adjusted her robe. In a few short hours, graduation would be over, and she would be free for the summer. As part of her improvement plan, she would be forced to attend three anger management courses over the break, so she wasn't completely free, but for the most part, she had escaped the year unscathed.

Arriving at the gym a short time later, she made her way inside and found her chair. She had never attended a graduation ceremony as part of the faculty, and found herself a bit nervous at the prospect. The district borrowed the facility from a local college to house the graduates and their families for the event, and she paused to take everything in.

On the floor level, rows of chairs stood in two halves, about six hundred of them, all facing the stage. Inside of them, lining the aisle down the middle, as well as the ones on the sides, sat more seats that were for the teachers. Locating hers, she clutched her robe and lifted it a few times at her bosom to swoosh the air through it; "Damn, these things are warm!"

Giving her an odd look, the teacher next to her turned away, and focused on something across the great room. Instantly, she knew she'd been snubbed. Of course, things had been tense since the whole cupcake incident had blown up in her face, and the rest of the faculty had gone from speaking to her very little, to totally ignoring her. *I don't know if I want to come back here after all,* she quietly admitted to herself. *Not if this is how it's going to be.*

Lining up a few minutes later, the ceremony seemed long and dull, and she found herself scanning the rows, searching for students she knew. Opening her program, she skimmed the names, mentally checking them off. *Well, overall, it was a pretty successful year*, she sighed to herself as the final name was called.

When the last of the students had filed out, and the staff were released, Becky felt like jumping up and down. Excitedly, she slipped off her robe and dropped it onto the back of her chair, as instructed. Heading out the exit on the far side, she climbed the stairs and walked briskly across the parking lot. Arriving at her car a bit out of breath, she paused, half aware that someone had called her name from behind her.

Pivoting slowly, she searched the throng of faces, jumping slightly when Jason presented himself in front of her; "Becky!"

"Hey, you!" she grinned, "I never would have thought you would be one I had to get onto about using my first name!"

"It's all good," he leaned against the car door she had opened, preventing her from closing it. "I'm legal now. All graduated, so we can be friends. Am I right?" his smile appealed to her, almost begging for her to agree.

"You know, hun," she patted him on the arm, "I appreciate that you feel that way; but I don't feel comfortable being friends with my students. Even after they've moved on." In reality, she had never met any of them after they had graduated, but this familiarity he held for her told her clearly enough; *we're not going to be friends, Jason.*

A look of disappointment flickered across his face, and for a moment, his expression bordered on angry. Her eyes wide, she feared he might actually tear into her, but instead he gave her a small smile, "It's ok, Miss Stewart. I get it. I'll see you around." Stepping back, he set the door free and walked away, visibly struggling to hold his head up after being publicly rejected.

Two weeks later, Becky sat at a table at a coffeehouse, pretending to read a book. She had been sitting there the better part of the day, glaring out the window at the hhgregg building across the strip. She knew that Jason worked there; at least she felt pretty confident that he did. She had heard him talk about it often enough, and had even seen him at that very cafe one night when she stopped to purchase a coffee.

"Hey, Miss Stewart, how's it going?" a male voice interrupted her thoughts.

Looking up, she found Mark's warm smile glowing down at her. "Hey, hun; how are you?"

"I'm good," he patted her on the shoulder. "You enjoying your summer?"

"Sure am," she grinned, showing him the cover of her book. "Would you mind getting me a refill?"

"Not at all," he grabbed her cup and headed to the back.

At that moment, Jason entered through the double glass doors and made his way to the counter. Flashing her his full set of teeth when he turned around, he made a beeline for her table and plunked down: "Fancy meeting you here."

"Hi, Jason," she squirmed.

"Hello, Becky," he chuckled, waggling an extended index finger at her when she looked to protest, "Nu-huh, I told you; you are no longer my teacher, and that makes us equals. I can call you whatever I like." Seeing that she wasn't convinced, he leaned back in the chair and held his hands up in surrender,

"Come on, whatcha gonna do? Send me to the office? I don't think so!"

His laughter intoxicated her, and she melted beneath his charm. She had spent days thinking about his farewell at her car the last time they had spoken; had been haunted by the idea that she had made the wrong choice. "Why do you want to know me?" she asked quietly.

"I like you," he held her gaze firmly. "I've had a bit of a crush on you since the first day of school," he admitted in a quiet tone. "But, since you were my teacher, I knew that it wasn't going anywhere," he shrugged, "So I settled for writing the day's agenda on the board for you."

"Really," she giggled, a warm flush creeping up her cheeks. Becky wasn't a virgin, and certainly wasn't a dewy-eyed school girl. She had always kept her relationships short, not wanting to become entangled in anything that she couldn't get out of. "I'm not sure other people would approve of our being friends... or anything else."

Taking her hand, he folded it between his, "I don't give a rat's ass what other people think. I'm ready to be all grown up, and I would love to take you to dinner. Just say yes," his warm smile enticed her.

Her brown eyes wide, she breathed deeply for a moment, formulating her reply. "Seriously, hun. It would be really complicated. I really think I should say no."

Unmoved, he stared at her, their eyes locked in a silent tug of war.

Licking her upper lip, she whispered softly, "We should take it slow."

"You're getting closer," his lips parted into a soft smile; "We've got all the time in the world. Say yes, Becky."

Her heart fluttered; *shit*. He wasn't going to let her go until he got his way. *What's one date going to hurt?* But deep down she knew, even sitting there just holding his hand could cost her everything if given the right twist. "Jason…"

"Say yes, Becky."

"Ok, one date. Yes," she exhaled loudly as she spoke, and a smile covered her face.

"That's it," he squeezed her digits firmly and leaned forward, planting a single gentle kiss on her quivering lips.

THIRTEEN

Payday

"PAY UP," Jason demanded, dropping into the chair between his two best friends. Rubbing his hands together greedily, he continued, "How much is in the pot, anyways?"

"Almost two thousand," Mark slurped his drink, "But who says you won? School's out already; nobody won. Not until next year, when we start college."

"Bullshit," Jason punched the other boy in the chest, "I fucked the bitch, and that was the bet. I won, so where the hell is my money?"

Cutting his gaze over at Alex, Mark waited for him to back him up, but the third young man only shrugged, "I'm not sure if it counts; the contract doesn't stipulate dates. If she were to get fired over the summer or at the start of next year, I would expect to get paid."

"It does too have dates!" Mark raised his voice, "You can't say it goes on after the year ends!"

"Maybe you could," Alex shrugged, "If any of the targets had acted and quit teaching between being selected and now, I'm sure you would call yourself the winner."

Mark narrowed his eyes at the other boy, knowing he was

right; if any of their previous choices had left the profession since being selected, he would take credit. "Fine. You can have the money, but you gotta prove that you did it."

Pulling out his phone, Jason lay the lighted screen on the table, "I got pictures."

"Oh, no!" Alex screamed, grabbing the device, then dropping as if it were on fire, "I can't believe you tapped that, man!"

"Hey, we all do what we gotta do," Jason cackled loudly, "And let me tell you, I earned that two grand."

"Hey, you know in a way, this is a victory for all of us," Mark lifted his glass in a toast, "We finally completed a contract." The trio laughed in unison, recalling their brilliant plan that had spanned five years, teachers and classrooms.

"Yeah, and it was fun," Alex agreed. "It made school a lot less boring. Although, I sure thought I was gonna get it this year when they yanked her in for poisoning us. I couldn't believe she didn't get fired over that shit."

"Hey, you had no proof that she did it," Jason defended, "Just like she couldn't prove we put the condoms all over her room."

Their hoots grew thunderous at the recollection of filling the latex tubes with squirts of lotion and tying them shut. Opening the door to her classroom after she left, the trio had distributed the packages around the cabinets and been out in less than ten minutes.

"Yeah, that was a good one," Mark clamped his friend on the back, while wiping at a tear that had spilled over from his jovial mood. "You guys are the best; I tell you. Anyways, I'll get the money for you, and you can have it. But I think we should change the rules when we get to college. I don't think getting them to quit or be fired will be nearly as easy with those guys."

"Hell, it wasn't so easy as we thought it would be, even in

junior high and high school. But, I agree," Alex nodded. "I think we should all get the opportunity to bang the bitch. Only we should pick good looking ones, not the pitiful looking cows or decrepit old spinsters we have been."

"Hey, Becky isn't really that fat," Jason, pointed out, "She just has that massive rack sitting on her chest," he held up his arms to represent her over-sized breasts. "And she's not old either. Anyway, I don't care. I won, and this is payday."

Continuing with their meal, the trio plotted their next move, all the while an uneasy feeling hovered in the back of Jason's mind. He had felt guilty that morning, snapping the pictures while the woman slept, and then slipping out before she awoke. He had never really thought about what it would be like if he actually won, but now that he had, the victory didn't feel quite as good or taste as sweet as he thought it would.

Chewing on his burger, he stared off into the distance, until Mark waved his hand in front of his face, "Hey man, what're you dreaming about?"

"Nothing," Jason shook his dark waves, swiping them out of his face. "I just hope she isn't mad that I left, or that I don't care about seeing her anymore."

"Don't worry; one night stands happen all the time. She'll wake up, and not give you a second thought," Alex laughed.

"Yeah," Mark agreed, "I don't think you need to worry about that. She'll suck it up and move on, either way."

Taking a long drink, Jason's mind continued to turn. *I hope you guys are right; she got pissed off enough to poison you,* he recalled to himself. Picking at his French fries, a feeling of dread crept up his spine. *Yeah, she's proven she could be a bit psycho; what if she doesn't move on, either way?*

FOURTEEN

Morning After

BECKY LAY in the early bright light, breathing deeply. Not daring to turn over, she knew Jason would be lying behind her, sound asleep. She knew it, because that's where he had been every time she had checked during the night. *I can't believe we did this... I did this.* She had let her wall down, and there was no going back.

It had been a crazy ride, ever since she had met Jason Truitt. In her classroom, he had been a handful, but at the same time, she had enjoyed his presence. She had maintained her professionalism, and she felt proud of that accomplishment.

Taking their relationship to the next level after graduation had not been an easy choice. Their first date had been filled with terror; fear that she would be recognized, and all the problems that would follow if anyone raised concern over her activities with her former student.

But he had reassured her every step of the way. Moving slow and true to his word, they had taken weeks to arrive where they now stood; *or lay, as the case may be.* She smiled at the thought, growing confident.

Rolling over, she was ready to face him. The next instant,

she felt hot tears on her face; *shit!* Sitting straight up, she buried her face in her hands, sobbing loudly, before she got a handle on her emotions. Sliding her feet to the floor, she made her way to the bathroom, where her shower awaited, and she cranked on the warm cascade full blast.

Standing beneath the spray, her lip quivered, "Why did he leave?" Her self-doubt raging, she could think of a few hundred reasons, and none of them good. Toweling off a few minutes later, she began to formulate excuses; *maybe he had a reason for not saying goodbye.*

Maybe he did, and I just don't remember it! Making her way to her closet, she selected a flattering blouse and a pair of jeans. "I think I'll visit him at work today. I can pop in and offer to take him to lunch." *That would be innocent enough.* She couldn't let it go, either way; she had too much vested in him to simply let him walk away.

Her primping complete, she slid into her car and rolled down her window to enjoy the breeze. Flying down the narrow freeway, she took the exit and turned into the parking lot of the shopping center that housed the electronics store. Easing her car into a spot, she opened and closed her fists a few times to fight their sudden need to shake.

Come on, relax, she coaxed herself. *He cares about you; you know he does.* There wouldn't be any reason for him to be so nice to her if he didn't; no reason to pursue her if it wasn't real. She had avoided romantic entanglements for so long. *It's time to take the plunge,* she assured herself.

Hoisting herself out of the car, she froze, her gaze falling on the outdoor patio to the cafe across the lot. At one of the tables, she spotted Jason, sitting between Mark and Alex; *holy shit!*

She wasn't even aware that the boys knew each other, much less that they were friends. Sliding back behind the wheel, she sank down in the seat, her mind reeling. Adjusting the rearview mirror, she could see them, talking and laughing, until another car pulled in and obstructed her view; *mother fucker.*

"What do I do?" she cried aloud to herself, her entire body beginning to tremble. Her emotions on the edge, she knew she hadn't done anything wrong; at least where Jason was concerned. *He's nearly nineteen years old, and no longer my student.*

Still, she couldn't shake the dirty feeling she got when she thought about having lain with him. What's more, she felt certain that no one else would see it that way. *Oh my God, I'm totally fucked; I've thrown everything away for nothing.*

Holding her position, she waited for them to split up, so that she could speak to her would-be boyfriend alone. Praying in the meantime that she had misread everything, she wanted desperately to believe that he did in fact care about her. However, she had to admit, it looked pretty grim.

Finally seeing him crossing the lot to his store, she flipped down the mirror and touched up her makeup. Then, grabbing her purse, she scurried after him; entering the store and following the front, she pretended to shop.

Working her way through, she had a vague idea of where she would find him. She knew that he handled computer issues, from the plethora of stories he had shared with her over the school year. *All those times he was pretending to be nice to me,* she seethed. *Calm down,* her better half argued; *you don't know anything yet.* Maybe all of this is one big misunderstanding. *Yeah; I bet.*

Arriving at a row of laptops, she inched along, opening and closing some to inspect the cases; *where are you, you little bastard?* Spying him next to the register, her heart began to pound. *Oh, God! I wanted it to be real,* she admitted silently to herself. *I'm tired of being alone; I'm tired of wondering if anyone will ever love me!*

Lifting her chin, she forced her lips into a smile as she approached, "Hey, honey!"

His eyes wide, his expression held pure terror, "Miss Stewart!"

Hearing the formal name roll off his lips, she closed her eyes, her emotions shredded. Opening them slowly, she held the smile, "When do you get lunch?" she asked calmly.

"I don't get a lunch today," he stammered, shifting from one foot to the other nervously, "I'm on a five hour shift, so I only get a fifteen minute break."

"Lovely," she agreed in a sweet voice, "That's all the time I need. I'll wait for you," she stated calmly, turning her back on him, and wandering through the store.

FIFTEEN

Denial

JASON WATCHED the woman working her way through his department, her pretty pink blouse flowing around her. Her honey brown hair hung in waves on her shoulders and down her back, and he thought again that she did make a nice looking woman; *despite what the guys think.*

Shaking himself back to reality, he helped customers with their purchases, and struggled to give clear and concise answers to their questions. In the end, he felt like a nervous wreck, waiting for the confrontation he knew would come in a matter of minutes. Eventually, his manager announced over the radio to go on his break, and he moved to find her; ready to face the music.

He knew he could slip out, and avoid talking to her, but he feared what she would do if he chose that path. *Man up,* he told himself firmly; *you managed to get into her bed, the least you can do is let her down easy.*

"Becky," he called softly from behind her, reaching out and patting her shoulder. He could see the stress lines on her face, and the smudges where she'd been crying. "Let's go somewhere private, please."

Leading her out the front of the store, he held up a hand, indicating the cafe across the street. Clutching her purse, Rebecca led the way, glancing at the black sneakers behind her as they followed.

"I was surprised you left without a goodbye," she managed in a weak voice once they were seated, thankful that they were alone in the afternoon sun.

"I'm sorry," he mumbled, "I didn't mean for it to be that way."

"Really," her voice became curt, "And what way did you mean for it to be, Jason?"

"Look, Miss Stewart," he stalled, "Becky, I mean; sorry," he swallowed hard. "Becky, I don't wanna hurt your feelings, but I don't think I'm interested in seeing you any more."

Her jaw dropped, she glared at him. "What's that supposed to mean?"

"It means, I'm done with you," he put it more bluntly, his patience wearing thin.

Her face instantly colored to a bright red, "What the fuck do you mean, you're done with me? You think this is a game? That I'm some little piece of trash you can toss aside whenever you feel like it?" her voice grew loud.

"Shh," he advised, wafting his hand at her, "I understand that you're upset. Furthermore, I can't say that I blame you," his Adam's apple bobbed again, "But seriously; this has gone as far as I intend to let it go. Now, you should hold your head up, and have some dignity about you. Give me a little wave when-ever we meet, and have that secret twinkle in your eye, from our special moment in time. You know, you don't have to ruin it by getting all pissy about it."

"Twinkle in my eye!" she breathed. Leaning forward, she stabbed the table between them with a stiff finger, "You listen to me, you little fucker, I told you; I'm not some little high school bimbo you can take to bed and then throw away like it didn't matter. This was real, God dammit!"

"It was real," he agreed with a small nod, "And it's really over." Standing, he leaned towards her, placing his mouth next to her ear, "Please don't, Becky. Don't make it hard; don't make a scene. If you do, then I have no choice but to get you in trouble. I don't want to do that; believe me. So, please don't make me."

Pushing him back so she could see his face, her voice shook with rage, "What the hell is that supposed to mean?"

"It means," his gaze fell to her perfectly painted lips, "That all I have to do is tell them you were after me… you know… and I have some things. Things you might not want other people to see."

Lightning quick, her hand shot up and landed against his face, "You lying little bastard!"

Holding the bruised cheek, he stood up straight, "I have to go. My break's over, and I think this is, too."

"Don't walk away from me!" she squealed, leaping out of her chair to follow.

"Stop!" he spun around, shoving a finger in her face. "You should go, and don't ever speak to me again. If I see you," his chest heaved, "I'll tell. And I'll show them the pictures I took of you."

His breathing erratic, he had lost his self control at her shocked expression, "Oh, yeah, I got proof, sweetheart. You like that job of yours, you better stay away from me, and keep your mouth shut. After all, who are they gonna believe?"

Turning on his heel, he marched away, leaving her in stunned silence. Reaching the glass doors to his shop, he weaved his way to the back, where he splashed cold water on his face before returning to the floor. All the while, his head spun, thoughts and memories of his senior year and Rebecca Stewart dancing in his head.

He had always heard that it was the greatest year of a person's life; that final one before becoming an adult. Too bad no one warned him that it could also turn out to be the worst.

SIXTEEN

Down Low

BECKY SLAMMED the door to her apartment, causing the walls to shake, while she screamed, "YOU LOW DOWN, MOTHER FUCKING, SON OF A BITCH!" at the top of her lungs. Snatching whatever was handy, she sent them sailing around the room; clothes, furniture and dishes landed against the smooth paint and fell to the floor in heaps.

Eventually, she arrived at the table that held her computer, and she froze, glaring down at it. The wheels turning, she flicked it on and sat down. Logging into vent, she found a few of her friends sitting in a channel. Swallowing to remove the anger from her voice, she asked quietly, "Has anyone seen K-nine around?"

"Nope, not today," one of the others offered readily, "But he's going with us on a raid tonight if you need to get ahold of him; he should be on later."

"Hey, thanks," she smiled to herself. "I'll be back later, then."

Logging off, she got to her feet and began to clean up the mess she had made in the midst of her rage. While she worked, she plotted. *First, I need to find out everything I can about those boys; all three of them.* That's where K-nine's help would come in handy. She didn't know his real name, but they had chatted enough, she knew he was a cop.

"He'll have access to records," she rationalized, "And he'll know what I should do next." The wheels turning, she quickly deduced she might want some help from the school side as well, but it would need to be discrete.

Her mind racing, she doubted going to Gary would be a good idea; he was her boss, but had proven to be a spineless twerp. Anna Marshall had been across the hall from her for an entire school year, and yet the two of them had spoken to one another maybe a dozen times. *Somehow, I don't think she'll be willing to hear or help me with this.*

Becky only briefly thought of Glenda Pritchard, laughing out loud; *hell, no.* No, she needed someone she could trust. Someone who had shown care for her, and given her good advice in the past. Instantly, her mind darted to William Carver.

Bill had been at her interview, when she put in for the transfer to Central High, and they had crossed paths many times since. As her mentor, he had a vested interest in seeing her succeed, and she had even been mildly attracted to his sense of humor and charm before she had discovered he had a wife and family.

Sighing loudly, she reached for her phone. Scrolling through the contacts, she located the number he had given her when he had told her to call him anytime she needed help. "Well, I hope this qualifies," she muttered, sending the call.

A moment later, a male voice responded from the other end, "Uh, hello?"

"Hey, Bill. This is Becky… Stewart. How's your summer?"

"Fine, I guess, only it hasn't started yet," he laughed. "I'm in administration, so I only get a couple of weeks, an' that'll be at the end of July. What can I do for you, Becky?"

"I need your help, Bill. Is there somewhere we could meet, and speak in private?" her hand trembled, causing the phone to bounce against her ear.

"Sure," he stammered at her ominous request, "Is my office ok, or do you need something away from school grounds?"

"Is away too much to ask?"

"No, not at all. I have to admit, there's been a few times I've needed to get more… one on one; if you get what I mean," his words gave her a chill.

"Ok, let's meet at the park, across from the courthouse. It's big, and we can remain out of sight, without really sneaking around."

"Sure, that's a good place. Five benches over on the green path; count from the main entrance. I'll be there in half an hour."

"Yes, sir," she giggled, an odd feeling of joy washing over her at the idea he really intended to help.

Taking her purse, she skipped down the stairs and rushed over to her car. Inside, she gripped the wheel tightly, and guided the vehicle to their meeting point. Locking her bag inside, she pocketed the keys, hoping that she appeared to be out on an everyday stroll through the beautiful greenery.

Arriving at the bench a few minutes later, she perched on the edge, noticing that Bill had arrived right behind her, and was sauntering up the walk. Once he was seated next to her, she began right away, "Thank you so much for coming. I know your time is very important."

"Of course," he smiled, leaning back on the wooden slats, "Relax, Becky. We're just here to have a little chat. Now, what seems to be the problem?"

"Well, as you know, I had some trouble this last year, with some boys. Actually, with one boy in particular; Alex Reyes," she paused, waiting for his nod of understanding. "Anyways,

there was another boy that something else has happened with…
has been happening with, only I didn't know - "

Holding up his hand, he cut her off, "Stop right there.
You're not about to confess something illegal to me, are you?"

Her eyes wide in horror, she shrieked, "Hell no!" Glancing
around, she dropped her tone, "I swear to you, I have never
done anything; not like this!" Guilt instantly flooded her
thoughts, and she sobbed, "I gave them a laxative, ok? They
spiked my water, and all that other shit, and since nothing was
ever done about them, I figured I might as well even the score."

Bill sat up straight, preparing to leave, "I'm not sure that I
can help you after all."

"Wait!" she grabbed his arm, tears staining her face, "One
of them tricked me. Only it didn't happen during school, I
would put my life on that! And I didn't even know they were
friends, until today, when I saw them together. Please, you have
to believe me," her voice cracked.

Studying her drawn features, the man inhaled deeply, then
spoke quietly, "Dare I ask who the other boy is?"

"There's two; Mark Covey is one of them. He was in Alex's
class, and I never knew they were buddies. And Jason Truitt is
the third," she said, almost in a whisper, noting that Bill's
eyebrow shot up at the last named suspect. "Do you know
him?" she frowned.

"Perhaps," Bill relaxed into the seat once more, his curiosity
back in full swing, "I can't give you details, but this is not the
first time that I have heard of these three boys in cahoots with
one another."

"Really!" she gasped, "Tell me!"

"I'm afraid I can't do that," he shook his head gently. "I
need you to give me the rest; you said one of them tricked you.
What did he do?"

"After graduation, Jason convinced me to go out with him.

We went on a few dates," the man next to her fidgeted as she spoke, and she hesitated. Her voice down to a whisper, she completed the thought. "Last night was our last one. We slept together, and this morning, I woke up alone."

The color drained from the man's face, "Are you kidding me? You had a sexual relationship with a student?" he struggled to keep his words between them. "Are you out of your damned mind?"

"No," she shook her head slowly, "He had me convinced that he was genuinely interested in me, and had been all year. Nothing happened before graduation, I swear it; but today, when I confronted him, he said that I better leave him alone, or he would fabricate a story and get me fired!"

"Jesus Christ," Bill covered his face with both hands, leaning against them with his elbows pressed into his knees. "Have you told anyone else about this?"

"No, not yet."

"Well, don't. This story needs to stay tightly contained," removing his digits, he clasped her on the shoulder, "Don't mention it to anyone; don't go around any of those boys. In fact, you should plan a vacation for yourself; go someplace that makes you happy, and get away for a few weeks."

"What are you going to do?" she demanded.

"I can't tell you that; we need to keep this on the down low. Again, you pretend like this never happened; not the stuff in your class, not the stuff with the Truitt boy; none of it."

"But he has pictures," her lip quivered.

"Don't worry about that," he reassured. "Go home, and pack; leave town tonight, and don't come back until it's time for in-service." Getting to his feet, he walked away, leaving her to follow his commands

SEVENTEEN

Home Sweet Home

"WELL, IF THIS ISN'T A SURPRISE," Emma Stewart greeted her only daughter on the front lawn, "Even after you called, I didn't really expect you to show up!"

"Aww, come on, mom!" Rebecca threw her arms around the older woman and hugged her tightly. Unexpected tears streaked down her face, "I should have come sooner."

"Yeah, you should have," Emma agreed, "But I'll take it. Come on in and get ready for dinner."

Inside, nothing had changed in the two years since her last visit; the one where she had buried her father. "Wow; it looks exactly the same!"

"Somewhat," her mother smiled, "Put your things in one of the guest rooms, and come down to the kitchen. I phoned your brothers, and we're gonna have a houseful tonight!"

"Oh, no!" Becky squealed, secretly elated that they wanted to see her. Climbing the stairs, she took the middle room, since it was the largest, and tossed her bags on the bed. Moving to the window, she stared down at the back yard, admiring the view.

Neat and tidy, five oversized oak trees stood in the open area, an old tire swing hanging from one of them. From the lack of grass and worn spot beneath it, she surmised that her nieces and nephews still used the device; "Wow. Home sweet home."

It felt odd to her, being in that place. She had never really enjoyed her family; at least not as much as the rest of them had enjoyed it. The only girl, with two older brothers, and one younger, she had always felt left out. So much so, that when she turned eighteen and graduated from high school, she had left home and never looked back.

Heading off to college as soon as summer started, she had gotten a jump start, and graduated with a master's degree four and a half years later. Striving to be the best, as she always did, she immediately took a job teaching ninth grade, and had been at it ever since. Or at least she had until this last year, when she moved to teaching twelfth graders.

Dropping the curtain, Becky made her way to the hall, and down the stairs. Her kids never had understood, nor appreciated, how hard she worked; or why she had pushed them so hard. Not ever intending to have a family of her own, she had looked at her students as if they were an extension of herself; the children that would never be hers, and she wanted it all for them. *And look where that has gotten me,* she sighed to herself.

Arriving at the kitchen door, she paused, taking in the space. "So, who's coming?"

"All of them," her mother laughed. "Afraid you won't stay more than a day, and they'll lose their chance, I guess."

Two hours later, the house swarmed with Stewarts; brothers, children and wives. Becky almost felt overwhelmed at their number, noticing that two of the youngest she wasn't even aware had existed. Joining the group for the meal, and sitting quietly to listen to them tell tales afterwards, she felt a pang of regret that she hadn't made the trip sooner. She fell asleep just before midnight, completely ecstatic.

The days passed quickly, and before she knew it, three

weeks had gone by. Waking up early, Becky lay in her bed and watched as the sun slowly filled her room. Blinking into the lessening darkness, she realized she had not thought of the school or her employment since her arrival. She had pondered Jason briefly a few times, but had managed to push him out as well, for the most part.

Shoving her hands behind her head, she stared at the ceiling, in awe that she had been so relaxed in the place she dreaded being most. Instantly, a wave of nausea twisted her gut, and she leapt off of the mattress.

Darting down the hall, the bathroom door banged loudly as she rushed inside and dropped to her knees in front of the toilet, spewing the meager contents of her stomach into the basin. A few minutes later, she flushed the rancid mess away, and moved to the sink, where she swished water around to remove the taste of the vomit.

"You ok?" her mother inquired from the doorway, as she watched her daughter wash.

"I'm fine, momma," Becky reached for a towel and patted her flushed cheeks. "Just a stomach bug."

Her mother grinned, "You didn't tell me you had a boyfriend."

"I don't have a boyfriend," Becky denied, but instant dread slapped her in the face, "Oh, shit!" Spinning around, her eyes darted about her for a moment, looking for something she might have lost; "What day is this?"

"Tuesday," her mother replied calmly.

"No, the date;" *oh my God, this cannot be happening!* Back in her room, she rummaged in her purse and pulled out her datebook; the one she used to keep track of her monthly cycle. *Holy shit!*

Glaring at the rows of boxes, her hand began to shake, causing the numbers on the page to blur. Sinking down onto the bed next to her, Emma grabbed a few strands of hair and tucked them behind her daughter's ear.

"Momma," Becky lifted her eyes to stare at her.

"It's ok, baby," her mother soothed, "It was bound to happen sometime. When do we get to meet him?"

Shaking her head slowly, the girl swallowed, "I can't say; I need to go home," she leapt to her feet, and began throwing her belongings into her bag.

"But I thought you were staying until time for school to start!"

"I was, but this can't wait," Becky located clean clothes to change into; "I have to get this taken care of."

"Taken care of! Now wait just a damned minute!" Emma's voice had grown loud, "You're not thinking of doing what I think you are!"

Pausing, Becky's brown eyes bore into her old and wrinkled features; *shit.* "No, mom, it's not like that. It's something else."

"Well, you make sure that it isn't. It's a sin; murder in fact, to harm an unborn child."

"I know, mom," Becky panted, pulling her shirt over her head. "Don't worry; I'll go see a doctor, and if that's what it is, I'll let you know." Standing up straight, she bit her quivering lip. She had never felt more trapped in her entire life, as if her world were unravelling around her and there was nothing she could do to stop it.

EIGHTEEN

Bystander

BECKY SAT in the waiting area, her legs crossed, with the left bouncing over the right. Having worn a dress, with hose and even high heels, she had attempted to make herself the epitome of professional in light of the situation she faced. Seeing Bill inside his office, moving around, she forced herself to breathe in slow and deep, then exhale in a similar fashion.

When he finally came to the door and signaled to her, she made her way inside, waiting for him to close the portal before taking a chair and perching on the edge of it; "I'm sorry to bother you."

"Don't be," he tossed a folder on the desk. "We've had a few minor setbacks, but I think we're going to make it through."

"Ok, so what's the plan?" she held her bit of news nervously, eager to hear what he had to say before she dropped the bomb on him.

"The plan is, you will be on an improvement plan. You're not to have private contact with any students, outside of class hours. All tutorials will be supervised, and you will not share the reason for this with anyone," he stipulated.

Sucking in air as if she had been stabbed, Becky leapt to her feet, "That's outrageous! I haven't done anything, God damn it!"

"According to Jason Truitt, you have. You have used your position as a teacher in an unprofessional manner, leading up to your encounter after the school year ended. This story is corroborated by several other students, including the two you mentioned previously, who have both also levied a grievance against you."

"This is fucking preposterous!" she bellowed.

"Sit down, Miss Stewart," Bill commanded.

Sinking into the chair, her mouth opened and closed several times, as if she were unable to actually inhale the air around her. Finally, she spoke in a much lower tone, "What else? How long do I have to do this? I should quit, or sue you guys, or something!"

"You may resign; but if you do, we will pull your teaching certificate for professional misconduct. This plan will last a year, and if you make it to the end without any further incident, then you'll be cleared," he closed the folder. "Since all of the parties involved have agreed to this, it really is your best option. I truly am sorry, Becky."

"Yeah, me too," she breathed. "When I came to you for help, I was thinking of something a little more in my favor."

"Under the circumstances, it's the best I could do," his features softened. "Know this, Miss Stewart; karma has a way of working things out. These boys will get what they deserve in the end."

"Not from where I'm sitting," she scowled. "From my point of view, the students get to prey on the teacher, while the administration stands around like a bunch of bystanders, allowing it to happen." On her feet once more, she clipped, "Do I need to sign anything?"

"Yes, please," he spun the folder and presented her with the pages, "And I have prepared a copy for you," he lay a sealed envelope next to her hand while she pushed a pen across the page.

"Gee, thanks," she snatched it up and stormed out of the room.

Outside, she stood on the steps of the administration building, the warm August sun on her face. Feeling lost, her steps down appeared slow, almost labored; as if it were painful to make each one. Reaching the sidewalk, she turned and walked down the street, making a left at the light.

A few blocks over, she arrived at the park where she and Bill had first met to discuss her situation. Locating the green path, she walked calmly along it, her heels clicking against the rough stones beneath her. Arriving at the fifth bench, she sat down and opened the envelope to see what their agreement actually said.

Reading the pages slowly, a few tears snuck out of her eyes and dripped onto the ink, causing it to blur. In addition to the tutorials situation, she would be closely monitored on her grading. Worst of all, she was not allowed any type of contact with any of the three boys in question. It could only have been worse if they had actually involved the police.

Allowing herself to cry for a few minutes, she calmly folded the pages and tucked them inside the envelope. The last stipulation would be the hardest to take; for not being permitted to speak to him, she could not ask Jason the most important question of all. Why? Why had he done this to her?

A moment later, she realized she had not informed Bill Carver of her condition. *Of course, that could be a good thing.* Unable to speak to her child's father, and knowing bearing an infant under such a strained situation would only cause more grief, she felt bound to end the misery before anyone else were able to discover it.

NINETEEN

Friendly Advice

"You ARE FUCKING KIDDING ME," TeeTops laughed into the mic, "That's the most absurd thing I've ever heard!"

"Hey," K-nine cut him off, "Listen, man, you don't repeat that shit to anyone; and you, HotStuff. You don't tell anyone what you just told us."

A stab of guilt shot through her, and Becky sighed heavily, "I won't; and I'm sorry that I involved you guys. But you're my only friends, and I could really use some good advice."

"Come on, we ain't your only friends," Tee carried on, "That would be messed up." A dead silence followed, as all three of them seemed lost in thought.

"Teach, you hear me over there?" K-nine tried again. "I'm serious; an' you know I'd never steer you wrong. Don't tell anyone what happened, and do what they tell you to do. No sense in you going to prison, or losing your certificate over some kid's crazy story."

Sniffing loudly, she watched his little icon light up as he spoke. Finally, she keyed her own mic, "I sure wish that I knew you in person," she confessed.

"Hey, you never know; maybe you do!" his laughter loud, it

gave her an instant chill. "I'm just kidding, girl; don't sweat it. Take care of that though, and get rid of all the evidence. And don't worry; your man Bill is right about one thing. Karma will take care of this."

"Yeah, I'm sure she will," Becky laughed, spitting slightly and reaching for a tissue. "Thanks again, guys. But I really need to get off of here and get some things done."

"Yeah, no worries, Teach," TeeTops replied, "We'll see you around."

Closing the connection, she didn't wait to hear K's farewell, broken-hearted all over again by her choice to reach out to them. *God dammit, there isn't a soul on this planet I can turn to.*

Rising from her chair, Becky changed her clothes and headed down the stairs. She had called and made an appointment for that afternoon, and it looked as if she were going to keep it. She knew what she had to do, and only prayed that God would forgive her. Of course, her mother never would; not if she ever learned the truth.

That's why she had come up with a great deal of false evidence to cover herself, ending with the miscarriage she would be having later that day. At least, that's what she planned to tell her mom.

Taking the bus so she wouldn't have to drive herself home afterwards, she sank into a seat and stared out the window. A short time later, a young woman came on board, with a tiny infant strapped to her chest. Noticing her, Becky quickly returned her gaze to the glass, but her eyes refused to stay put, and darted back to her to steal glances at the top of the small head.

Finding herself staring at the soft wisps of hair, she frowned heavily. Her mind slowly turning, she thought about the fetus she currently carried inside her. She had referred to it as a fetus every time she spoke of it, never wanting to think of it as an actual person.

Forcing her eyes back to the road, she recalled that she had never wanted to be a part of a long term relationship; had never wanted a child of her own. *But what if I've changed my mind?*

Her thoughts growing distant, Becky considered her options once again. Of course, she could have a child of her own, even without a man. *I could adopt; I could get it artificially done, with a sperm donor.* If she did that, the father would never know about his child. *Just as Jason doesn't know about this one.*

Instinctively, her hand moved to her stomach, and her fingers splayed across it. *I'm right at twelve weeks; they say the worst part is behind me,* she thought of the morning sickness that had plagued her. Glancing at the young woman again as the bus rolled to a stop, she could see the sign to the clinic on the opposite side.

This is it, she instructed herself. *Time to get up and go take care of all the evidence, just like K-nine suggested.* Somehow, she couldn't bring her legs to move; couldn't force herself to stand. Instead, she remained there, until the doors had closed, and the bus rolled forward once again.

Riding the loop, she arrived back at the stop near her apartment some time later. Exiting the massive transport, a peace settled over her; an idea that things were finally going to be the way that she wanted them to be. Climbing the steps to her tiny home, she let herself inside, ready to head up to the school. There, she would begin to put her room in order and prepare to face the new year.

TWENTY

Examine the Evidence

SCOOTING into the desk next to a girl with long dark hair, Rebecca grinned, "Looks like I still fit."

Giggling, the girl agreed, "Yeah, Miss Stewart, you're not that big, yet." Adjusting the page so the teacher could see it, she pointed out the questions she wanted to discuss.

Listening to her, Becky felt as if she had died and gone to heaven. Her new students seemed polar opposites of those that had gone before them, and as her belly grew, so did her faith in humanity. Digging deep and preparing the best lessons she could, her kids had thrived, and begged for more. Thrilled with her life to the depths of her being, she had never been so happy.

Being the beginning of the third six weeks, which fell just before Thanksgiving break, she had become perfectly accustomed to the restrictions that had been placed upon her. In an effort to conceal the need for her supervised tutorials, she and Anna Marshall had become tutoring buddies, and had both groups of students meet in one room or the other.

One of Anna's students, the girl she currently assisted, needed help with a different subject; but Becky had a firm grasp on the material, and was prepared to do her best. "First off, tell me your name, so I'm not calling you 'girl' the whole time."

Giggling, her braces glinted in the florescent light, "I'm Brittany Truitt."

"Brittany," Becky repeated, her breath caught in her throat. *Truitt; oh, no!* Resisting the urge to pry, she turned her attention to the questions and they went over each one in turn.

A few minutes later, Brittany commented offhandedly, "I think you had my brother, Miss Stewart. He'll be home for Thanksgiving tonight; he should come and see you."

"Oh, no; I don't think so," she replied quickly, trying to stand and becoming hung on the desk for a moment before she made it to her feet. "I don't recall any Truitts. No need for him to visit," she grinned to cover her dismay.

Giving her a shrug, the young lady placed her page inside her notebook and tucked it safely inside her backpack. "Anyways; thank you for the help," she called over her shoulder as she left the room.

Casting her eyes around at the empty desks, Becky noted that everyone had been helped and sent on their way. Gathering her things, she turned to Anna to discover that the woman glared at her disapprovingly; "What?"

"Why did you lie to that girl?" Mrs. Marshall demanded.

"I don't know what you're talking about," Becky denied, backing away and preparing to run.

"You did too know her brother; I had him three years ago, and you had him last year."

"Oh; I must have forgotten," she had made it to the exit and darted across the hall, an odd feeling twisting in the pit of her gut. "Jesus Christ," she breathed, dropping onto her chair and laying her head on the desk for a long moment.

Ready to leave a few minutes later, she made her way out to her car and home, hoping that nothing more would come of it. Back at the school the next morning, her nerves had calmed, and she didn't give the incident a second thought, until the end of third period, when someone knocked on her door.

"Jacob, can you let them in please?" Miss Stewart called from the back of the room, where she aided a group with their project. Turning a moment later, she found herself staring into the face of none other than Jason Truitt.

"Hi," the slender young man spoke in a strong, level voice.

"Uh, hi," she stammered, her hand instinctively tracing the line of her belly.

Catching the movement, his eyes dropped, taking in her changed shape. Licking his lips, he shoved his hands into the front pockets of his jeans. Choosing to wait until they were alone, he moved to lean against the board.

Glancing at her clock, Becky swore under her breath, "Guys, it looks like we're out of time. Take what you have home, and bring them back finished after the holiday, so we can make our presentations." She wanted to look around as she spoke, to ensure that they were following directions, but she couldn't take her eyes off of the man before her.

At that moment, the bell sounded, and the room erupted into a moment of chaos as the students gathered their supplies and bolted for the door. "Have a good holiday!" she called after them loudly; "Be safe!"

"Be safe," Jason chuckled, mocking her as he moved towards her.

Lowering her chin and cutting her eyes up at him, Becky clicked her tongue, "What's that supposed to mean?"

"Oh, I dunno; not sure that you've ever cared about your students before," he wafted his hand around them, taking in the emptied room, "What makes these guys any different?"

Shaking her head, she moved to her desk and grabbed her

lunch bag, "I don't have time for this. I have to eat; tutorials start in twenty-five minutes."

"Ah, tutorials; those were the days, right?" he lunged forward, catching her arm and preventing her from leaving. "Why didn't you tell me?" he growled.

"First off, there's nothing to tell," she yanked her appendage free. "And secondly, even if there were, you can't have it both ways, Jason." Taking a step back, she put a bit of distance between them. "Get out, before I call security."

"Call security," he scoffed, "And tell them what; you want your baby's daddy removed from the premises?"

The color drained from Rebecca's cheeks, "Shut up! You have no idea what you are talking about! You are NOT the father of my child, and what happened between us is a sealed secret; per your request," she reminded him,

"Oh, I'm not the father? Then I guess you won't mind if I ask for a paternity test, so we get that in writing. I wouldn't want any nasty little surprises popping up somewhere down the line," he sneered.

"You can't!" Becky shrieked. "I mean… that is totally not necessary!" *Shit!* Her mind racing, she took another step back, the desperation dragging her features into a heavy frown.

In two quick strides, he rendered her efforts moot. "Shut up! You and I both know that you're lying, ok? Just like you always have. I don't know what you did to these kids; you put blinders on them somehow, and they think the world of you. But I know who you really are; I know what a terrible teacher you are."

Pushing against his chest, her bottom lip quivered, "That's a lie; I'm a very good teacher! It was you boys that made things so hard last year. And you knew all along that they were making it hard on me… what they were doing to me." A tear escaped, and rolled down her cheek, "What I don't understand is why. How could you be so cruel, Jason; pretending that you cared for me, when you didn't?"

His eyes dropping to her belly for a moment, she thought he might be going to go all soft on her, and beg for forgiveness. Instead, he tightened his jaw, and hissed, "You have no idea who I am, do you?"

When she failed to respond, he adjusted his hold on her arms, squeezing them until she squealed in pain. "I'm a Truitt," he seethed. "We're the richest family in this fucking county. We get and do whatever the hell we want." Giving her a violent shake, he leaned down so that his face lay only a breath above hers, "Now; lie to me again and tell me that baby isn't mine."

"It isn't yours," she whispered. "It's mine. Now, get the fuck out of my classroom!"

Releasing her, he laughed, then spun on his heel and marched towards the door.

Bet Me

HER MIND RACING, Becky knew she needed help. The problem was, she didn't know who would stand behind her, or up for her, as the case may be. Grabbing her coat, she darted down the hall, bursting into Gary's classroom, "I need you to get my afternoon covered," she demanded in a rush.

Taking in her disheveled appearance, he stood with his lunch sitting before him, "Why? What's happened?" He unconsciously looked at her stomach, presuming it had something to do with her pregnancy.

Tracing the line of her rounded from, she shook her head profusely, "No, I'm fine," she smiled briefly, "Something else has happened, and I have to go; right now." Not waiting for him to deny her request, she flung the exit wide and darted down the hall.

Arriving at her car, she tossed her jacket and lunchbox in first, then slid in behind the wheel. Throwing the car into reverse, she whirled the wheel around and spun the tires for a moment before taking off across the gravel. Out on the highway, she pointed her car towards downtown, and prayed that Bill would be in his office when she got there.

Fortunately, she could see him through the open door when she arrived. Pushing past the woman trying to detain her, she slammed it behind her, and screamed, "You have to help me!"

Seeing the pure terror in her eyes, he indicated one of the guest chairs; "Please, have a seat, Miss Stewart," and made his way to the door. Waving off his secretary, he informed her, "I'm sorry, Liz, I made this appointment myself. That's it, no need for security." Closing the door a bit more gently than she had, he pivoted to look at her before demanding, "Ok, what's going on?"

"Jason came to the school today," she blurted, "He just found out that I'm pregnant, and he wants a paternity test."

"Right," Bill stroked his chin, "You know, we had a conversation not three weeks ago, an' you assured me that baby wasn't his."

"I lied," she stated bluntly, "Now, what the hell are we going to do about it?"

"You lied?" he bellowed, his arms shooting straight up into the air above his head, "How the hell could you do such a thing, Rebecca? Do you have any idea who that boy is? What you're up against?" He allowed the appendages to fall, slapping to his sides. "My God, his name is Truitt! Truitt, Rebecca! The same as the boulevard; same as the hospital wing; same as the elementary school. Are you out of your God damned mind?"

"I didn't know," she shrugged helplessly. "I didn't know about any of that."

"Well, it's not going to matter," he ran his hand roughly through his hair; "Those people own half this town. It was his idea to keep your involvement hush-hush; my take was that he really didn't want to drag your name through the mud. But this," he indicated her body with both open palms, "This will be hard to sweep under the rug. What are you planning on doing with it?"

"With what?"

"With what? With the baby - with what?" he laughed out loud, "Jesus Christ."

"Well, I'm keeping it, of course! It is mine, after all; he didn't want me, and he certainly didn't want a child with me, so why should this change anything?"

"Because, it just does," he flopped down in his chair and picked up the phone. "If you have anywhere you can go, you should run," he advised. "I'll try to salvage your name, but if that family gets their hands on you, I guarantee you will lose your rights to that infant; you mark my words."

"No," she reached across his desk, hanging up the line, "Not until you tell me what I need to know. You knew something was wrong; that day in the park. You weren't surprised by what happened! Tell me!"

Laying the receiver in the cradle, Bill looked as if he'd been beaten. His jaw hanging, he collected his thoughts for a moment. "If I tell you, not a word of this leaves this room, you understand?"

Dropping into the chair, she breathed, "Tell me."

"Three years ago, when those boys were sophomores, we had another teacher come forward with many of the same complaints that you did. Only instead of putting condoms in the drawers, they toilet papered the inside of her room. It was the same routine, pretty much play by play."

"Fuck," Becky blurted.

"No, it didn't go that far, but it wasn't for a lack of trying." Bill chuckled anxiously. "I guess he got a lot smoother over the years, or she had a lot more insight. She wasn't fooled by his advances, and she went to administration to file a complaint against him, for sexual harassment."

"Oh my God, you are just now telling me this!" Becky leapt to her feet.

"Sit down," he instructed, "And calm down while you're at it; you're not doing that baby any good." He leaned back in his chair and ran his fingers over his face, "Anyway, we handled it in house; the records were sealed, and nothing ever came of it."

"Ok, so who was the teacher?"

"I can't tell you that," he stared at her calmly, but he could see the wheels turning.

"Holy shit, it was Anna Marshall, wasn't it?" she was on her feet again.

Shaking his head slowly, Bill sighed loudly, "You didn't hear that from me. Now, here's the kicker; these boys were doing this as some kind of wager. Some pool they had going, where they picked a teacher each year. Each of them put the screws to her, and depending on the outcome, one of them would win the kitty."

"And how do you know this?" she demanded curtly.

"It came out in the investigation. They needed one of three things to happen; you to quit, you to get fired, or you to end up in bed with Jason Truitt. I guess he finally collected the pot."

TWENTY-TWO

Broken

"I NEED SOME COFFEE," Detective Browning pushed his way to his feet, looking down at the young woman before him. "You wanna walk around for a minute? I'm sure that chair isn't doing your back any good."

"Thanks," she stretched as she joined him. "Actually, I could use a little girl's room again; and another cup if you care to grab it for me."

Showing her down the hall, he left her at the entrance to the bathroom and went on to his office. Pausing next to his partner's desk, he stated flatly, "She's clean; she's told me the same story three times, and she hardly changed a word of it. And if she knows the person responsible, she hasn't made the connection. We're going to need some fresh leads to follow."

Detective Andrew Martin leaned back in his chair, shoving his hands behind his head, "Well, you know, it was a bit of a stretch to begin with; thinking she could drag two full grown men around and dispose of their bodies. Not to mention pregnant."

"Yeah, but she's the most likely suspect; and she had the

most to lose if those guys got their way." Turning to the coffee pot, he stepped back out in the hall, "Becky," he caught her when she came out, and motioned her his way. "We're gonna let you go. I don't see any reason to detain you any longer."

"Really?" she smiled up at him, "Well, thanks, I think!" Turning, she paused, "Where's my purse and stuff?"

Shooting his partner a quick glance, he guided her down the hall, and instructed her to wait outside. "You don't want anyone in the lobby to see you," he cautioned quietly.

"Why not?" her eyes grew wide with a mixture of surprise and fear.

"Word got out that you were being questioned," he exhaled loudly as he spoke, "So it's packed with reporters."

Her mouth dropping open, she instantly perked up, "I want to speak to them!"

"What?" he took a full step back, "Are you crazy? You can't go out there!"

"Then set it up; there has to be a room around here some-where that we can use." When he looked as if he were going to deny her request, she lunged towards him, poking him in the chest, "You're the one who said I could leave! Now, you either get me a place or I'm going out that door!" she pointed at the exit over his shoulder.

Holding up his palms in surrender he grunted, "Ok, go back to my office and have a seat. I'll gather your personal effects and figure out where you can hold a press conference."

Reluctantly, Becky retraced her steps, until she came to the wide office filled with several desks. Seeing Detective Martin seated at one, the name plate opposite it read *Browning*. Moving quietly, she tiptoed across the floor and slunk down into Albert's chair.

"So, when do you suppose Truitt's body will turn up?" the man didn't look up as he spoke.

Stunned, Becky began to gasp for air noisily, "Do you really think Jason is dead?"

His face shooting up to stare at her in surprise, Andrew stammered, "Oh my God; I thought you were Al!"

"Obviously not," tears spilled over and ran down her cheeks, her heart broken at the idea that Jason might be lying in a ditch somewhere. "Is he missing?" *They hadn't said that he was; only Mark and Alex!*

"I'm... really not at liberty to discuss that with you," he hesitated, realizing he had made a major error.

"Not at liberty to discuss what?" Browning asked from over his shoulder.

"He said that Jason is missing!" Becky leapt to her feet, "Is that true?"

"He's still unaccounted for," Albert admitted quietly. "We aren't sure what that means yet; we do have people searching for his body."

Heaving ragged sobs, she burst into loud wails. Moving towards her, Detective Browning pulled her against his broad chest and ran his large hand firmly down her spine, "There, there," he soothed. "It's ok. You have enough to worry about without adding the likes of Jason Truitt to your plate."

"You don't understand," she sniffled loudly, "I made this baby with him; I loved him!"

The two men exchanged a solemn glance, and he squeezed her tighter before releasing her. "Becky, I strongly advise you again, not to speak to the press. In your condition, it would be a recipe for disaster."

"No," she dabbed at her eyes, "I need to do this. I need to get the truth out there."

Opening his mouth, Browning looked as if he had more to say, before he closed it slowly. Deep down, he knew he couldn't stop her, and in the end, her appearance might give their case the break they were looking for. "Right this way," he ushered her towards the door.

TWENTY-THREE

Obvious Conclusion

LEAVING THE SMALL RAISED PLATFORM, Becky tried to smile. She had done her best to convey her sorrow at the loss of her former students, via a small statement. She had also pled for the life of the third, if he were in fact still alive, and asked for his safe return from whoever had him.

Afterwards, she had fielded questions, and the orderly gathering had quickly descended into a frenzied bloodbath. The detective had been persuaded by her story, but obviously the public at large would be much harder to convince, and drew its own conclusions. Either way this worked out, her career as a teacher was more than likely over.

Her heart heavy, Becky made her way through the back hall, where she gathered her jacket and purse from the detective's desk. "You headed home?" he asked her in a quiet tone.

"No," she shook her head, "We're on holiday, and I'm going to visit my mother; my brothers and their wives... kids." She ran her hand absently across her round stomach, and the baby turned beneath her touch. "You know, when I first found out I was pregnant, I didn't even want it."

He noticed that she didn't look at him when she spoke; "Oh?"

"No," she gave him a weak smile; "I guess it grew on me."

Grinning at her presumed pun, he chided, "Get some rest, Becky."

"Yeah, I will," she said goodbye with a little wave. Showing her out the back way, Detective Martin led her to her car, and she climbed in. Making her way home, she felt numb; the pain had crashed in around her at the idea that Jason might be gone, paralyzing her ability to think beyond the moment.

Upstairs, she packed her suitcase, and headed back down to her car, where she tossed it in the trunk. Back behind the wheel, she pointed it towards her momma's house, turning on the radio to take her mind off of the trouble that swirled around her. Two hours later, she pulled into a small convenience store, and made her way to the bathrooms in the back.

Picking up a few snacks, she stood in line at the counter, observing the growing dusk through the large plate glass that covered the front. "Wow," she mumbled to herself, "Maybe I should have waited until morning to leave on this journey." With another eight hours of road ahead of her, she knew pushing on would be a dangerous decision.

Her turn, she dropped her items in front of the clerk, and asked quietly, "Is there a motel or anything like that around here?"

"Sure," he gave her a small nod, scanning the packages as he spoke, "Stay on the service road, and you'll come up on it about half a mile down the way."

"Thanks," she handed him a twenty and waited for her change. Backing out of the lot, she noticed a fiery red sports car tagging along behind. When it didn't take the on ramp to the highway, she felt her palms grow sweaty.

Pulling into the motel, she parked right at the front door,

beneath the lights; ready to make a dash for the entrance. To her relief, the red Firebird passed behind her car and drove to the end of the row, parking out of sight. "Wow, you've got yourself all worked up," she giggled quietly as she peered at the neon vacancy sign.

Inside, it only took a few minutes to secure her quarters, and she parked in front of her room on the other side; exhaustion taking it's toll. Lifting her bag out of the back, she waddled towards her room, setting the alarm and taking comfort in the quiet beeps. Swiping the keycard against the lock, she twisted the knob to step inside, when a man came out of nowhere, shoving her in and closing the wooden panel behind her.

Throwing the privacy lock into place, Jason straightened himself to his full height, glaring down at her as she turned to face him, "So; where are you running off to?"

"I'm going home to my momma's house," she replied softly, feeling as if she had been tricked somehow. "You weren't kidnapped, were you?" her voice flat calm, it sounded disappointed.

"Who said that I was?" he demanded loudly, and for the first time she noticed the pistol in his hand.

"Shit," she muttered under her breath. "I guess once again, I get to play the fool." Her suitcase on the floor where she had dropped it, she hoisted it onto the table.

"Yeah, you do," he raised his hand, waving it slightly at her. "You know, I don't understand how a lady as smart as you could be so stupid."

"I trust people," she grimaced. "That's how."

"You're full of shit," he held the gun firm, "It was a nice little speech you gave, though. Especially that very heartfelt plea for my safe return."

"You saw that?" she flopped the suitcase open, her back to him, hiding her pained expression.

"Yeah; I saw that," he laughed. "You know, at least part of the time, I actually did like you. But then you turned out to be like all the rest."

"Like all the rest," she frowned, searching for her sleepwear in the near darkness. "And how am I like all the rest?" Locating a tee shirt and boxers, she dropped them onto the chair, her fingers fighting the buttons on her blouse.

"All you cared about was my family's money," he bit through clenched teeth. "Why else wouldn't you tell me that you were pregnant?"

Becky gasped, "Because I haven't seen you since I found out; and then they dragged me in and made me sign that stupid paper, saying that I would never have contact with any of you! From what I understand, that was your idea, so who's fault is that?" She didn't look at him, her anger at the young man rising.

Watching her top fall to the floor, Jason could see the rounded curve of her silhouette. Staring at her changing shape, he swallowed. "I don't believe you," he hissed. "And why the hell are you taking your clothes off?" he demanded, giving the gun another shake.

"Well, don't," she clasped her maternity pants and pulled them off as well. "Don't you recognize pajamas when you see them? I've been at a police station for two fucking days, being interrogated. I'm going to bed."

Down to her undergarments, she pulled the boxers over her panties and slipped out of her bra. Covering her swollen breasts and belly with the thin cotton top, she turned to the queen sized mattress and sighed.

"What the hell is the matter with you? Some guy breaks into your room at gunpoint, and it doesn't even bother you? You just strip off your clothes like it's no big deal?"

"I guess it depends on the guy," she pulled the covers over

her as she stretched out. "My God, that feels good." Curling into a ball facing the far wall, she felt on the verge of tears.

The room had remained dark the entire time, only the light from the window illuminating it. No longer able to see her, he held up his hands, allowing the pistol to hang from a single finger in frustration. "You're crazy, you know that?"

"Well, you should have figured that out the night I slept with you," she countered, her voice muffled slightly by the pillow. "I mean; think about it. I risked everything that I was for a single night with you. What person in their right mind does something like that?"

"Risked everything," he mocked her. "And how's that?"

"Even though you were old enough, and no longer my student; the rumors would fly. It wouldn't have ended well, and either way, I would have a broken heart. It was the obvious conclusion to our relationship; I either lost you, who I loved, or my job, which I also loved. There was no winning for me, after that first date; after that day you convinced me to say yes."

TWENTY-FOUR

Stand Your Ground

STARING DOWN AT HER, able to make out her honey curls in the dim light, her words left him numb. Laying his pistol on the nightstand and kicking off his shoes, he stretched out beside her. Taking the top side of the covers, he lay flat on his back and stared at the ceiling above them. "Nobody cares if we were together," he informed her.

"They're going to fire me," she corrected him quietly. "The press will run stories and make up whatever they want. Former students will come forward, and it will be over; regardless of the truth."

Rolling over, he placed his hand on her shoulder. Feeling the tension in her muscles, he kneaded her flesh. Moving to her back, he pushed against her, causing her to moan. "You like that?" he asked her quietly.

"It feels good," she admitted, rolling halfway onto her belly. "I'm exhausted from sitting in a stiff chair all day."

Taken with the need to comfort her, he worked her muscles, getting onto his knees and using both hands. Her groans guiding him, he massaged the lower part of her back, then pulling back the covers, he applied pressure to her buttocks and thighs.

When he had finished, he stood, removing his jeans and tee. Joining her between the sheets, he snuggled up behind her. His arm draped around her, his hand rested upon her belly. "I'm sorry," he mumbled into her hair. "I never thought of it that way. Without my input, it never occurred to me that they would do anything to you."

"It doesn't matter," she sounded tired, on the edge of falling asleep. "I'm going home to my mother's house. I can stay there until my baby is born; and go from there."

"Our baby," he corrected, his hand pressing gently on her, the baby kicking him through her abdominal wall.

Biting her tongue, she chose her words carefully; "Whatever, Jason." When he didn't respond, she felt angry. "You should go; I don't need you here."

"You don't need me, huh," he pushed himself up onto his elbow and glared down at her. "But do you want me here?"

"No," she shook her head and wiped at an escaped tear at the same time. "You wanted your freedom, and you got it. I can do this by myself, and I really wish you'd go away."

His fingers digging into the flesh of her shoulder, he pulled her onto her back. "Look me in the eye and say that shit to me," he clipped, his voice strained. "I'm trying to make things right between us, Becky."

"Then put your fucking pants on, and get the hell out of my room," she bit through clenched teeth.

His jaw hanging open, he glared at her through the darkness. "I don't get it; you said you loved me. You told the press you wanted to see me safely returned."

"Yeah, I did and I do. But wanting you to be safe doesn't mean I need you in my life. I've got this, Jason. It's my baby, and my responsibility. We don't need some kid hanging around, playing daddy whenever he feels like it," her lip quivered. "It takes a man to raise a child, and I'm sorry, but I'm not sure that you qualify."

Throwing back the covers, he leapt to his feet, anger surging through him. "You fucking bitch!" he paced back and forth, squeezing his hands into fists.

Gripping the comforter, she pulled it up to recover her tired frame. Rolling onto her side, she faced the window, tucking the blanket beneath her chin so she could watch his tantrum.

"What do you want me to say?" he demanded. "What do you want me to do?" Pausing his steps, he faced her. "Name it."

Blinking up at him, her words shook, "I asked you to leave."

"Well, fuck you, I'm not doing that. You don't wanna be my girl, that's fine. That's still my baby."

"You can't have it, Jason," her tone grew tense. "You're not taking it away from me!"

"You - " his voice caught in his throat. "You think that's what I want? To take it from you?" Tears filled his eyes, and he looked at the ceiling above him, blinking rapidly and cursing under his breath. "I would never do that to you. Our baby needs you; needs both of us."

Regaining his composure, he grabbed his pillow off of the bed and tossed it on the floor. Opening the drawers to the dresser, he located an extra blanket and stretched out on the carpet, draping it over himself.

"What the hell are you doing?" she scooted over and glared down at him.

"Go to sleep, Becky. We're both tired, and need to get some rest. Maybe tomorrow we'll be in better condition to work this out."

"Why can't you get your own room?"

Cutting his eyes over, he peered up at her, fear seizing his lungs. He was afraid she would run, and take his baby with her, but he couldn't say that. He'd already said too much, calling her names and pointing a gun at her. "Why'd you say yes?"

"Say yes?" she sounded perplexed.

"That day I asked you to go out with me; at the coffee shop. I kept insisting, until you caved in. Why didn't you stand your ground and walk away then?"

Blinking at him, she hid her smile with the edge of the mattress while tightening her grip on the sheets. "It wasn't an accident that I was there," she confessed quietly. "After I turned you away at graduation, it bothered me; like I had missed my chance at something important."

He swallowed, taking in the tiny revelation; "And?"

"And I was working up my courage to walk over to your store to look for you. But you came into the shop, and you know how that turned out."

"You wanted to go out with me," he deduced. "You liked it when I called you Becky," his lips parted into a grin.

"Yeah," she breathed a small laugh. "It felt so odd, the mixture of happy and dread. I'm scared, Jason. You were right; I didn't know who you were. If I had... I think I might have walked away."

Sitting straight up, his face stopped inches from hers, "What do you mean? You don't like my family?"

"I don't like the idea of them," she sighed, her hand sliding forward and brushing against his hair. "People who feel they're better than everyone else, who can do whatever they want."

Catching her hand, he toyed with her fingers. "I said that to you, didn't I."

"Yeah."

"I've been a real dick."

"Yeah..."

"Tell me how to make it better, baby," he leaned towards her, his breath on her face. "Or sleep on it; I know you're tired."

"I'm ok," she tugged on his digits. "I don't think I could sleep with this hanging between us."

"I swear, I'm not better than you. You're the kindest, most patient person I've ever known." Lifting his face, he touched his lips to hers, fireworks exploding around him the instant they made contact.

Getting to his feet, he pushed her onto her back, pulling the covers off of her. Stretching out over her, he could tell instantly that she wasn't comfortable with his weight pressing down against her belly. "I want you," he whispered, his voice choked.

Rolling, he reversed their positions, her hair falling down and covering her face as she languished over him. His hand tracing her neck and line of her jaw, he caught the brown cascade and pushed it up and out of the way so he could see her.

Staring down at him, Rebecca's heart began to pound. From the moment he had pushed his way into her room, she had been fighting the urge to put her hands on him; battling her desire to hold him and tell him everything would be ok. Her face only inches above his, she could see the need in his eyes, and feel the hardness of him beneath her.

"Jason," she breathed, her hand pressed against his muscled chest.

"Yes?" he softly hissed.

"I don't care if they fire me," she held her position, ready to confess. "I don't care what anyone else thinks. I would choose you all over again; I do love you."

His smile cut a long dimple into his cheek, and his fingers massaged her scalp. "Well, you're on top, so you're in charge. Are we making love, or getting some sleep?"

Dropping her mouth to his, she tasted him, biting gently at

his lips. "Actually, I think we're gonna do both," she whispered against his neck, her fingers tantalizing his skin.

"Hmm," he searched for the hem of her tee, ready to remove the clothing she had donned a few minutes before. "Yeah, miss," he teased, "By all means... have your way with me."

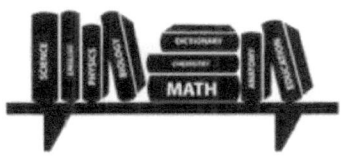

TWENTY-FIVE

Down and Dirty

JASON RAN his fingers lightly over Rebecca's soft skin. Planting a gentle kiss on her bare shoulder, he smiled; "Good morning."

Catching his fingers, she squeezed them lightly; "Good morning, yourself. Did you sleep well?"

"Yeah," he leaned closer, breathing lightly across her ear. "I have to admit, this is not how I pictured all of this working out."

"It hasn't worked out, yet," she reminded him, rolling onto her back so she could look at him.

"What do you mean?"

"Well, someone murdered your friends," she reminded him in a soft tone.

Staring at her for a long moment, he blinked back his anger. Finally, he managed in a rough tone, "You think I did it, don't you."

"Baby, I wouldn't be laying here if I did," she soothed, her fingers sifting through his hair. "The problem is, the cops are going to think the two of us are in this together; at least I'm betting they are."

"How do you figure?"

"That detective made me tell him the story; the whole thing, start to finish three times. Then, he let me go. I'm fairly certain he figured I would lead them to you."

"Oh, shit!"

"Yeah, and here we are, in bed together. I have this fear that when we open that door, it's all over."

Sitting up, Jason peered through the tiniest of cracks between the curtains, then turned back to her, "I love you, Becky. You have to know that. But, if I'm taking the fall for this, there's no way I'm taking you down with me."

Her hand brushed lightly across his chest, "Make love to me then, and forget about what's outside. At least for the time being."

Catching a hint of movement through the crack, he rolled off the bed. "Sorry, baby; but I can't do that right this second." Grabbing his jeans, he army crawled to the bathroom, and didn't stand until he was safely inside. "Stay there," he called to her softly. "They may come busting in, so don't panic."

"What are you going to do?"

"I'm going out this window. My car is still parked on the other side of the building. Maybe they haven't noticed it yet, and you can stall them while I get away," he pushed against the lock, working it back and forth until it was free.

"So, you're just going to leave me to them," she sighed, not sure how she felt about that.

"Yeah, baby. It's time to get down and dirty. We have to find out who's really behind this, because we're fucked if we don't. Like you said, everyone wants to see us as the bad guys, even if we're not."

"Ok," she could feel her confidence growing, "Are we meeting somewhere?"

"No," he pushed up against the pane, "Go to your momma's. When I get this worked out, I'll come for you; I promise." Sliding through the tiny space, he felt amazed that he had fit through it. Outside, he glanced up and down, noting the row of weeds that grew behind the motel.

An instant later, his shoes and shirt dropped out the window. "There's your stuff," she called quietly, "And I'll see you at mom's," she whispered loudly before closing the glass and starting the shower.

Picking up the shirt, he tugged it over his head. Then grasping the shoes, he discovered she had shoved his pistol into one of them. "Well, she is a smart lady," he mumbled to himself. His feet covered, he dove across the narrow strip cf bare ground and forced his way into the brush, collecting a few cuts and scrapes in the process.

It took him the better part of an hour to work his way around to the side cf the motel where his car sat, and by that time, he had decided they had been wrong about the cops. However, since their plan was in motion, he felt disinclined to alter it. Climbing into his fiery red sports car, he started the engine and flew out of the parking lot, headed for the highway and back to town.

In the room, Becky had soaked for a long while, allowing the warm cascade to relax her tired muscles. She had been exhausted after her long hours of interrogation, and wasn't looking forward to being back in police custody.

Eventually, she cut off the spray and used a soft fluffy towel off the rack. Patting herself dry, she smiled at the thought of the night they had spent together. *At least we got the chance to set things right between us.* She had hated the thought of his never knowing that she had truly loved him; *but now he does.*

The idea immediately saddened her a little, and she knew their situation had actually changed very little. *If Jason isn't able to figure out who's responsible for the deaths of Alex and Mark, it's highly likely we won't ever see each other again. Or, more likely, I'll be paying him conjugal visits after he goes to prison.*

Getting dressed, she caressed her belly affectionately, "Don't you worry sweetie; mommy and daddy are gonna figure this out." Lifting her bag off the table, she drew a deep breath, and reached for the door handle. Her fingers lying lightly against it, she allowed the air to escape in a slow hiss, as she prepared to face the officers who would be outside.

Flinging the door open, she waited for them to appear. When nothing happened, she poked her head out, and looked up and down the walk; *well, I'll be damned.* Closing the portal behind her, she scurried over to her car and tossed her bag in the back seat. Behind the wheel, she pulled out, stopping at the office long enough to announce she was leaving, and then she got out on the open road; headed for home.

TWENTY-SIX

Pick a Path

TEARS STAINED Rebecca's cheeks as she drove. Sniffing heavily, then wiping at them with an old paper towel, she could not stem the flow. Jason had left her to ensure she would be safe, and had gone into the fray to clear their names.

Pulling up in front of her mother's house, she calmly collected her bag and made her way to the door. Feeling odd, whether she should knock or go straight in, she decided on a mixture of both and poked her head inside, calling loudly, "Mom?!?"

Emma Stewart came to the top of the stairs, "Becky?" Taking a few of them, she paused again, "What're you doing here?"

Meeting her at that point, the younger woman's flood gates opened wide, "Oh my God, momma; I'm so happy to see you!"

Hugging the girl, Emma demanded, "Why didn't you call and let me know that you was coming?"

"Well, I didn't know that I was," Becky admitted, guiding her mother down the stairs and into the kitchen. "But every-thing has turned out so crazy, and I'm afraid that things are bound to get worse before they get better."

Sitting down at the table, she wanted to explain what had been happening in her life; to share her pain with someone she knew would care about it and her in the end. Watching her mother flit around for a moment, she asked quietly, "What are you doing, momma?"

"Getting ready for Thanksgiving dinner, of course; it's tomorrow. I thought that was why you were here," she laughed at her only daughter, confused by her strange behavior.

Before they could take the conversation any deeper, a ruckus picked up in the front of the house, and the pair moved back into the room to discover Becky's oldest brother, Matthew, had arrived with his wife, Karen, and their four kids. Karen gave the older woman a quick peck on the cheek, holding some covered dish suspended in front of her, before heading straight into the kitchen.

"Matt, what're you doing here? Shouldn't you be at work?" Emma smiled broadly, hugging her grandchildren and then shooing them outside.

"Naw, they kicked us out early at the plant, so we decided to come over an' help you get ready for the big day tomorrow. You know, our brood is gettin' a little big around here," he gave his sister a wink.

"Oh, Matt," Rebecca squealed, throwing herself into his arms and clinging to him for dear life. Sure, telling her mother about her problems would be cathartic, as the older woman cared; but telling Matthew would be something entirely different. *Matt might actually be able to help.*

Holding him close, she whispered in his ear, "I need you, big brother. Can we find a place out of the way, so I can tell you what's going on?"

Pushing her away so he could look her in the eye, he queried, "Are you in some kinda trouble?"

"No," she managed a small smile, "But someone I love very much is."

"We're gonna leave you two to the cookin'," he called to the women in the kitchen, "An' I'm gonna take my baby sister for a ride. We'll be back in a bit." Clasping her hand, he tugged her through the front door and loaded her into his SUV. Slapping the hood on his way around, he climbed in with a loud laugh, "Remember when we used to take daddy's ol' truck an' disappear for a few hours... usually when you had some guy that needed his attitude adjusted?"

"Yeah, I remember," she chuckled, snapping her seatbelt. "You always were my muscle, weren't you, Matt." Heaving a deep sigh, she nervously reached for the dash, then lay her hands across her belly. "We're in trouble; me and Jason. He and two of his friends did some pretty terrible things in school, and both of them are dead."

Cutting his eyes over at her, he raised his brow, "How old is this boy?"

"He's nineteen," she supplied calmly, knowing the question was coming, and probably would be for the rest of their lives together. "He and I started dating after he graduated," she tacked on for good measure.

"Ok," he gave his head a shake, "How'd they die?"

"Someone murdered them," she teared up once more, only this time she was ready, with her napkin in hand. "We don't know who, and we're afraid the police aren't going to help us."

Pulling into the local Sonic, Matthew ordered two large cherry limeades and killed the engine. Turning to her in the seat, he patted her on the leg, "Well, don' you worry now, sis; we're gonna take care o' this the best we know how. So come on, an' tell me all about it."

Only pausing when their drinks arrived, Becky spilled her

guts for the fourth time in as many days, leaving out no detail, and even added the information she had learned from her night with Jason. When she reached the end, she sat silently, waiting for her eldest sibling's evaluation.

"We need to find the other women," he provided after a few minutes of thought.

"What other women?"

"The ones they was pickin' on," he shifted in his seat. "It's either them, or someone close to them, that done it."

"How do you figure?" she breathed, unsure how he had come to that conclusion so quickly.

"Aww, sis," he laughed, gripping the steering wheel for a moment, "Imagine you was tellin' me this story, an' those boys had hurt you; maybe ruined your career. I could hurt 'em; bad. Kill 'em," he shrugged, "Maybe." He cut his eyes over at her, "Where's he at?"

"I don't know exactly," her breathing became shallow, "He went back to town, to try and figure this out."

"You got his number?"

"Yes," she grabbed her phone, and began to scroll through her list of contacts, certain she still had it from when they were dating. Locating it, she paused, "Should I call him?"

"No," he snatched the device from her, and started the engine. "I'm takin' you back to mom's. I'll pick up John, an' maybe even Luke. It'll take us all night to get there, but we'll do what we can."

"Jesus," she leaned her elbow against the glass, holding her head in her hands. "Mom's gonna be so pissed if you miss Thanksgiving dinner on account of me."

"Naw, she'll understand," he slapped her on the knee again before reclaiming the wheel and maneuvering through the traffic, "We all gotta pick our path, sis. I think she'll be more happy that you finally found yours."

Climbing out of the vehicle, it surprised her that Matt didn't even go inside with her. Instead, he peeled out of the drive, presumably to retrieve his brothers and leave her to do the explaining. Trudging inside, she made her way to the kitchen to do precisely that.

TWENTY-SEVEN

Out for Justice

"HEY, baby. Did you make it to your mom's place?" Jason answered the incoming call calmly.

"Yeah, she made it," Matthew chuckled into his sister's phone, giving the man seated next to him a wink.

"Who the fuck is this?" Jason's tone switched in an instant.

"Relax; I'm Matt... one o' Becky's brothers."

"Oh," the younger man exhaled loudly, "Thank God. You scared the shit out of me. Why're you calling, and not her?"

"Cause, she gave me her phone, an' we're comin' with you. I got Luke an' John with me, an' we're headed your way."

"Luke and John," Jason repeated absently, still groggy after being awakened by the call. He then recalled Becky telling him that all of the Stewart family had been given biblical names. "Right; brothers. Ok, when will you be here? I'm sleeping in my car and staying out of sight at the moment, so I'm pretty mobile."

"We're comin' into town now, so just tell us where to meet ya."

Giving him the directions to the coffee shop where Mark

had worked, he added, "Don't go inside. I'll be sitting in a red Firebird, out on the corner. That way we can all ride together."

"Tha's a good idea," Matt agreed. "I'll pull up next to you in a black SUV, an' you can hop over in the back seat."

"Roger that," Jason ended the call and put the car in drive, only a few blocks away from the rendezvous point.

Pulling into the shopping center, Jason's hair briefly stood on end. *It's after six am; this place should be crawling with the morning crowd.* Making a slow loop around the massive parking lot, he only noted a few cars, all empty and looking to have been there at least overnight. *Crap; it's Thanksgiving.* No one would be around today.

Choosing a spot out close to the edge, he leaned his seat back and removed his seatbelt. Adjusting himself into a comfy position, or as comfortable as he could get, he closed his eyes to continue his nap until Becky's relations arrived.

Coming from a rather large family himself, with four older siblings and one younger sister, the couple had exchanged family tales in detail during their dates. Recalling what Rebecca had told him about the three men he would soon meet, he felt an odd sense of excitement and wore a tiny grin.

Suddenly, a loud bang shattered the silence, along with the window next to him. Jolted back to reality, hands gripped the front of his jacket, lifting him out of the seat and yanking him out through the opening.

"What the fuck!" he screamed, flailing his arms about wildly.

Laughter answered his cries, as blows landed against his torso. The large pair of brown boots blurred in their swift attack. "So, you think pickin' on old ladies is fun... you little bastard."

Rolling over, Jason made it to his feet. "Wait... wait!" he held his arms out, blinded by the blood running into his eye.

"Jesus Christ, man!" A sharp pain pierced his belly and he howled in agony. Dropping to his knees, he felt the blade slashing at his throat, cutting a deep gash in his cheek before it hit the mark.

Holding the wound in his gut with one hand and his neck with the other, he curled into a ball. Dimly aware of a scuffle and that he was no longer under attack, he could hear the voices around him. *My God, they made it.* A moment later, he blacked out.

"Nine-one-one, what is your emergency?"

"Hey!" Luke screamed, clinging to Becky's phone, "I need cops an' an ambulance, right now!"

"Yes sir, what is your emergency?"

"Look bitch, a man's been stabbed, and his throat's cut! He's bleeding like a stuck pig, so can you send someone the fuck down here?"

"We ain't got time for that," Matt knocked the phone out of his hand, "Open the back!" Hoisting his blood soaked body, he lay Jason in the back of his Suburban, "Make sure that bastard don' go anywhere!"

"He ain' goin' nowhere," John kicked him again, as his captive struggled to free his zip-tied hands.

Peeling out of the parking area, Matt flew down the deserted streets, "Hang on back there, buddy." He knew Jason had been unconscious when he lifted him into the back, and his heart pounded at the thought of telling his sister they hadn't been able to save him. "Just hang on," he repeated more quietly.

Spinning into the ambulance entrance at the hospital, he was met by an orderly, loudly announcing "You can't park here!"

"Who the fuck's parking!" he shouted back, flinging the back door open, "I got an injured man here!"

A gurney was produced within seconds, and Jason shifted

onto it. Pushed through the sliding glass doors, he would be getting the best medical care available. Wiping at his face with blood soaked hands, Matt exhaled loudly, on the verge of angry tears from the rush of adrenaline.

Looking around, he felt lost; unsure what to do for a moment. Realizing he couldn't stay where he was, he climbed into the driver seat and pulled his freshly stained SUV around to the parking tower. Making his way into the hospital through the visitor's entrance a few minutes later, he located a bathroom and removed what he could from his hands, arms and face.

Moving back to the lobby, he pulled out his phone. He had several calls to make, and decided to save the hardest one for last. Pulling up Luke first, he needed to know that the boy's attacker had made it into police custody before he met with an unexpected end. "Hey, what's going on?"

"The police have the guy in the back of their car now," Luke informed him.

"Good, we're at that hospital we passed on the way into town. Shoulda known when John pointed it out, it was a bad omen. You boys headed to the station or coming over here?"

"John's talking to them now; we'll let you know."

Ending the call, Matt stared at the device; *fuck.* He hated to call his only sister, especially in her condition. "I could wait until we have an idea if he's gonna make it," he debated with himself. He knew that was a risk though, and that she would want to be there, either way.

Dialing his mother's house, he cleared his throat noisily; "Hey, mom. How's it going?"

"We're getting dinner in the oven now. You boys gonna make it back in time, or do we need to plan a late supper for you?"

"I really can't say," he winced, aware that his mother

remained in the dark about most of what had been going on. "Is Becky around?"

"Yeah," she agreed, holding the handset out to her daughter.

Taking it, Becky grinned at her mother's antique device, her fingers twirling the cord instantly out of habit, "Hey? Did you find Jason ok?"

"Actually, we found him. But there's a problem, sis."

Her heart froze instantly in terror, images of a young man's mutilated body flashing through her mind. "No!" tears spilled over, pouring down her face.

"Becky, we don't know anything yet. He was attacked, an' I got him to the emergency room. I thought I should let you know… in case you wanted to come down here."

Her hands shaking, she didn't reply, dropping the receiver and allowing it to bounce around against the wall and floor. Pulling off the apron that covered her round belly, she wiped at her damp cheeks.

"Rebecca Diane, what has gotten into you!" her mother called after her, while reaching for the cord.

Purse in hand, Becky exited the house and climbed into her car. Swinging it around, her shoulders jerked and her hands trembled. Bellowing into the empty space that surrounded her, she did the only thing she knew to do; she drove.

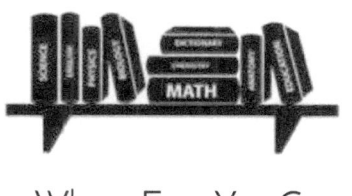

TWENTY-EIGHT

Where Ever You Go

"WE'VE LOCATED THE STEWART WOMAN," a uniformed officer informed the group from the door of the conference room.

"Good, is she in custody?" Detective Albert Browning demanded.

"Yes, they're going to load her into a helicopter, and she should be here shortly. Her car is being impounded by the local authorities."

"This meeting is over," Albert informed the others. "Be sure they take her straight over to the hospital. She's going to be a wreck."

"Are we going to interrogate her again?" Detective Andrew Martin used long strides to keep up with his partner.

"No," Al clipped, "She's been through hell, and it's not over yet. As soon as Pritchard is released, we'll be digging into him, although he doesn't have to say much."

Making their way out to Martin's car, the pair rode over to County Memorial in a strained silence. "You think he'll pull through?" Andrew finally spoke up.

"No idea," Browning toyed with his lip while his elbow rested against the window. "Damn unlucky, or pure stupidity, going over to Mark Covey's job site in that flaming red sports car of his. It was like a neon sign shouting, *hey, over here!*"

"He's just a kid; he didn't know any better."

"Well, it was plain ignorant. Thank God that girl's brothers got there when they did, but he still might not make it," the detective exhaled loudly.

Pulling into the parking garage, Andrew chose one of the VIP spots and hung his tag in the window. "He'll make it. He didn't die in the first few hours, so that's a good sign."

Strolling across the street and entering the building, they presented their ID's and were allowed access to the back elevators. Stepping out onto the right floor a moment later, they were greeted by a swarm of people in the small waiting room.

"What's happening?" a loud voice demanded.

"Are you the detective?" a second called from behind them.

Holding up his hands, the senior officer calmed them, "Everyone, please; I'm Detective Albert Browning and this is my partner, Detective Andrew Martin. We've been working this case since the first body was found, six days ago, and I assure you; we are doing our best. We do have Jason's attacker in custody, and we will be getting details to you as we are able."

The group remained crowded around the pair, but the voices faded away as he spoke. Continuing, he nodded, "That's more like it. Please; everyone remain calm..." The elevator opened and a uniformed officer escorted Rebecca Stewart into their midst.

At the sight of the familiar faces, she began to sob, "What the hell is going on? No one will tell me anything!"

Reaching for the young woman, Browning clasped her upper arm and guided her through the double doors leading to the back, while Martin dealt with the boy's family. Stirred up by the young woman's arrival, he could tell it was going to be a long day.

"Becky, we don't know anything yet," Al dropped her appendage and lay his arm across her shoulders. "He's out of surgery, and upstairs in a recovery room. When he's ready, they'll bring him down here."

"Who were all those people? Is that his family?"

"Yes, those are his relations. Apparently, he had gone into hiding not long after coming into town for the holiday, and that had them spooked. They had filed a missing person's report on Monday, which I'm sure you're aware. That's the day you were taken into custody and questioned."

"Yes," she sniffed, wiping at her tears. "You held me for days, grilling me, as if I would do anything to hurt any of those boys!"

"We had to know what you knew," he defended. "It's not magic, you know. We don't just wake up in the morning, and know who we're looking for. We have to find leads; and follow them."

"Who did this to him?" she asked quietly, her nails digging into her palms as she struggled for control over her emotions.

"The guy your brothers subdued at the scene is named Alan Pritchard; we'll be questioning him as soon as we're able. He's not as bad as Jason, but he's banged up."

"Pritchard!" she gasped, "Jesus Christ!"

Noting her response, he frowned, "You know him?"

"No, not exactly, but Glenda Pritchard works at the school with me. She's a teacher down the hall," she replied in a dazed tone.

At that moment, a pair of orderlies turned the corner, wheeling a bed in their direction. Covering her face with her hands, Becky's body began to shake, her sobs muffled. Watching with wide eyes, she could see the bandages covering his neck and cheek. Black and blue splotches decorated the flesh that was not hidden. "Oh, dear God," she whined helplessly.

Holding her firmly, Browning breathed into the top of her head, "Relax; we're gonna get you a few minutes with him before they let the family back here."

"Is he awake?" she asked the doctor as he approached.

Wafting a clipboard at her, he hesitated, "Not yet. But it's still early. In a few hours, we'll know more." Holding up a hand, he ushered her inside. "You may remain with him, if you like. We're keeping the family out for now, but Detective Martin assures me you have clearance."

"Clearance," Becky repeated softly, her hand tracing the line of her growing belly. "I guess you could call it that."

Sliding a chair over to the head of his bed, the glare of sunlight peeked through closed blinds behind her, giving the room a warm glow. Lifting his hand, his fingers appeared swollen, and several cuts there were stitched.

"Those are defensive wounds," Browning informed her. "He put up a fight; but an unarmed man against a surprise attack with a knife is a tough deal."

Caressing his exposed cheek, a tear spilled over and dripped from her chin; "Did you know that we saw each other after you released me?"

"No, I did not," he stiffened. "When was this?"

"After I left the station, I went by my apartment to pick up clothes and headed to my mother's house. I stopped at a motel on the way, and he had followed me," she sighed. "We talked for a few hours, and had decided we wanted to at least try to make a go of it." She rubbed her belly, feeling the gentle kick of his child.

With a small smile, she admitted, "We thought you would have followed me, and were going to arrest him. Now I kind of wish you had; he would have been safe, then."

"It never occurred to me that he would meet up with you," the Detective lamented. "He was never a suspect, and was always viewed as a potential victim."

"Excuse me," Detective Martin called from the door, "I hate to interrupt, but we've got some things to discuss," he waved a folder at his partner.

"Ok," he nodded in his direction. "Becky, I have to go. We're placing two officers outside this door; one of them is for you. If you go anywhere, he goes with you. You understand?"

"But... you got the guy," she looked up, her eyes glazed in fear.

"We got a guy; who he is exactly remains to be seen. Remember; officer Blevins goes wherever you go. Understand?"

Giving him a reluctant nod, she returned her attention to the patient between them. Exhaling loudly, the Detective left the young woman and moved briskly to the door.

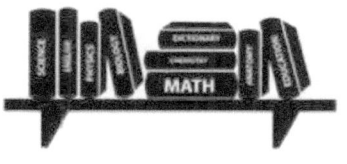

TWENTY-NINE

A Woman Scorned

"OK, LET ME HAVE IT," Browning growled, holding out his hand for the file.

"These are the records from downtown; the school district released them about an hour ago. Our three victims were implicated in an incident involving three teachers, a few years ago." they turned a corner and entered the back elevator before Martin continued.

"Mark Covey, Alex Reyes, and Jason Truitt were running some kind of betting pool. That's concrete. The rest gets a little iffy," he concluded.

"Alan Pritchard connected in any way?"

"Yup; his mother, Glenda Pritchard is named as the first victim. She was one of their eighth grade teachers, and they harassed the hell out of the poor old woman. The next year, it was Donna Haney, and the one who filed the actual grievance was Anna Marshall," the door opened for them on the ground floor.

Outside, Browning opened the folder, "I guess getting into trouble didn't stop them."

"Well, apparently not. We don't know if there was a victim

from their junior year, but I'm sure Rebecca Stewart was the last," Martin frowned, rubbing his brow. "It's a real shame to see the results; her career is basically over."

"Yeah, that's a shame, indeed. The press is going to have a field day with this," he smacked the page. "Why the hell didn't they bring the police in on this?"

"Because, it's bad publicity. They have always liked to handle things in house if they could get away with it. Honestly, I think a lot more goes on over there than we ever get wind of," Andrew speculated.

"Well, this isn't right. It says here, the first incident involving Stewart is her poisoning her students with cupcakes; according to her, it began months prior to that with her being bullied!" He sighed loudly, slapping the pages shut, "Let's get out of here. Get organized, and prep to interrogate Pritchard. We need to find out if the worst is behind us, or yet to come."

Upstairs, Becky allowed her tears to drip unchecked. She had been hopeful after Matt had left that everything would work out; especially with her oldest sibling there to look out for him. It broke her heart that he had come too late, and Jason had nearly been killed, and still might not survive.

A short time later, a nurse entered the cramped space. Looking over his chart and recording a few readings on the monitors, she spoke up in a firm voice, "They are going to allow the family in soon; I've been asked to advise you to wait elsewhere."

Cutting her eyes up at her, Becky sighed, "I don't have anywhere else to go, do I?"

"There's a waiting room on every floor, and a large one on the ground level; I suggest you choose one of those. Go to any nurse's station and give them your name to let them know where to locate you. We'll let you know when anything changes," she informed her before exiting the room.

Kissing his cheek lightly, the young woman complied. *The last thing I want is a confrontation with his family.* On her feet, she paused outside the door to inspect the name badges on the chests of the uniformed men; "Blevins?"

"Yes, ma'am," the tall black man smiled, exposing his brilliant white teeth.

With a small nod, she asked meekly, "How do we get out of here without going through the waiting area?"

"Right this way, ma'am," he reached for her arm, guiding her to the back side of the wing. Using the stairs, they went down one flight, and from there were able to get onto an elevator unscathed.

In the ground-floor lobby a short time later, Becky spied her brothers, all grouped in a corner. Her new bodyguard in tow, she made her way over, "Well, at least you guys are ok," she frowned at the bumps and bruises. "Nice shiner," she tried to smile at Luke's black eye.

"Thanks," he scowled, "That was one tough son of a bitch. Clocked me as soon as we interrupted him - "

"Don't," Matt cut him off. "I'm sure the last thing she wants is a blow by blow," he scooped her into his arms. "You ok, sis?"

"Yeah," she clung to him, her arms tight around his broad shoulders. "I got to see him, and I think he's going to make it. How it's going to work out remains to be seen." Loosening her grip, she smiled up at him, "Thank you for coming to help him."

"You betcha," he patted her on the arm. "We should get us something to eat."

"It's Thanksgiving day," John lamented. "Where do you suppose we can get lunch?"

"I know a place; it's expensive, but they're serving dinner for the holiday," Officer Blevins offered.

"And who are you?" Luke demanded.

"I've been assigned to look out for Miss Stewart," he informed them, shaking their hands. "You can call me Mack."

Sharing introductions, the group made their way out to the parking garage and Matt's awaiting SUV. As soon as they opened the doors, the smell of aged blood greeted them.

"Oh, God!" Becky stepped away, "I'm going to be sick."

"I'll get us a vehicle," Blevins informed them. "Wait back downstairs by the main entrance."

"You're not leaving me, are you?" Becky's voice grew shrill.

"Uh, no, ma'am!" he smiled down at her, "I'm right here behind you. Just gonna radio for a car to be brought over to us."

Making their way back down to the entrance, the three brothers placed the girl in the center, forming a diamond with the fourth man as they moved along. At the gate into the garage, they waited until the car arrived and Mack drove them across town for a good meal.

Arriving back at the hospital a couple of hours later, Becky nervously checked in on the ground floor. "I'm here for Jason Truitt. My name is Rebecca Stewart, and I was told you would give me information if it were available."

Pulling up Jason's records on her computer screen, the young woman smiled, "Yes, ma'am. Actually, they're expecting you in Mr. Truitt's room right away."

"Oh, dear God!" she breathed, gripping the counter for support. "Is he ok?"

"Yes, ma'am," she nodded. "He's been asking for you."

Her heart pounding out of control, a fresh swarm of tears flooded her eyes and spilled onto her cheeks. Spinning to face the men who watched around them, she announced, "We need to get up stairs, right away!"

Inside the elevator, she bounced slightly at the knee, "Holy shit; he asked for me!" Looking up at Matt, she grinned, "He's going to be ok!"

"Yeah," he shrugged, returning her smile with relief, "It's all gonna work out, sis!"

Leaving her three siblings in the waiting area, along with a large number of Truitts, Becky and Mack burst through the double doors and walked briskly down the hall. Arriving at the room, Mack joined the other officer outside, while the girl pushed against the wide portal.

Inside the small room, six faces turned to glare at her, causing her to pause. In the bed straight in front of her, Jason lay flat on his back, staring at the ceiling above him. Standing frozen in place, she stared at his profile until he moved, and then she squealed, "Jason!"

"Becky?" he immediately twitched.

"Lie still, son," his father commanded, taking a step closer.

Accepting the near side of the bed, Rebecca reached for his right hand, mindful of his IV. "Oh my God," she squeezed him gingerly.

"Hi, beautiful," he cut his eyes over to look at her.

"Ah, I'm afraid I don't qualify at the moment," she wiped at her streaked makeup. Her smile broad, she leaned over him, whispering loudly, "I'm so glad you're alive."

"Yeah; me, too!" he raised his left hand, catching a few locks of hair and tugging on them. "I'd like you to meet my parents," he wafted in their direction. "This is Terence and Genevieve Truitt."

Giving the girl a stiff nod, the couple did not appear eager to make her acquaintance. Her eyes on the rounded belly the girl sported, the older woman announced loudly, "Kids, why don't you give us a few minutes in here."

Standing to the side, Becky observed as Brittany and three other of Jason's siblings exited the room, looking her up and down as they passed by. As soon as they were gone, she dove in first, "I'm sure you were surprised to hear about me."

"Surprised is not the word we would use to describe it," Terence Truitt replied crisply, "So, we want to nip this in the bud. We will offer you fifty thousand dollars now, and an additional fifteen thousand a year until the child is twenty one."

Stunned, Becky squeezed Jason's hand, "Offer me... for what?" *Are they trying to buy my baby?*

"They want you to go away," the younger man supplied.

"Absolutely; this whole affair is outrageous!" Genevieve spoke up. "You should be ashamed of yourself, preying on a young, innocent boy! You are a teacher; you are trusted with the lives of children!"

Her mouth hanging open, Becky held no reply. Struck speechless by the audacity of the other woman, she could feel the color rising in her neck and face.

"See? I told you she wouldn't take it," Jason quipped, chuckling slightly.

Exchanging a glance, the older couple stood up straighter in unison, and his father laid down the law. "That's fine. I'm sure the pair of you will do well on a teacher's salary; if they don't fire her."

"What's that supposed to mean?" Jason glared at him, struggling for an instant to sit up before he rested back against the pillow in pain.

"It means, you will be removed from the household and struck from the will. We won't tolerate this; if you insist that your relationship with this woman continue, then ours has come to an end," Genevieve informed him crisply. Making her way around the bed, she exited the room, her husband following closely behind.

THIRTY

Family Ties

"PLEASE TELL me those really aren't your parents," Becky breathed.

"What?" Jason studied her from his reclined position. "What do you mean, not really my parents?"

"I mean, how could they be so cold? So cruel?" she squeezed his hand.

"They're just looking out for the best interest of the family," he observed, noting her drawn features.

"Well, to hell with them!" she cut a brief laugh, "I promise you, my family will be much more supportive," she leaned over him, her gut twisting "You're really going to be ok, right?"

"Yeah," he held her fingers as firmly as he could muster, "*We* are going to be fine. I'm really sorry about everything that's happened; I'm not proud of the things that me and the guys did. I swear to you, I'm going to make it right... for both of you."

"Excuse us," Detective Browning knocked lightly on the door, pushing it open, "We need to get a statement from this guy."

Nodding, Becky smiled, "Sure. I'll be in the waiting room

when you're done." Making her way out, Mack tagged along behind. Exiting the swinging doors, she gasped, "Where did everyone go?"

"They cleared out," Luke informed her. "Boom, all gone!"

"Wow, that's unbelievable!"

"What is?" Matt stepped forward, ending his call.

"They disowned him," she sounded breathless. "Just like that, they severed their ties."

Gaping at her, he demanded, "Dare I ask why?"

"Because of me," her face contorted. "They wanted to pay me off; to go away and leave him alone."

"No shit?" John reached over, pulling her against him, "And he refused?"

"Yeah, of course he did," a few tears escaped and ran down her cheek. "I can't believe they would do such a thing!"

"Well, don't let it bother you, sis," Matt squeezed her arm. "We were in here with them all of fifteen minutes; you woulda hated them," he laughed.

"Stop that, it's terrible!"

"I'm sorry; I was joking. Anyways, mom and Karen have arrived in town. They'll be here shortly," he informed the group.

"What about the kids?" Becky shook her head, "What about Thanksgiving dinner?"

"Postponed; we'll do it after Jason's out of the hospital," John agreed.

"Wow, this is all so… surreal," she patted her belly where a tiny appendage appeared to be stabbing her in an effort to escape.

A few minutes later the two women joined them. Sitting down on the cushioned seats, the group discussed all that had happened, until Albert and Andrew joined them.

"You guys can go back in now," Detective Browning announced.

"Thanks," Becky got to her feet, "Is everything squared away?"

"Well, yes and no," he shoved his hands into his pockets, "We're pulling your body guard here," he indicated Officer Blevins. "It appears that Alan Pritchard was working alone. He had a vendetta against the three boys who had harassed his mother while he was in prison. Paroled only a few months ago, he's been waiting for them to come back into town from college so he could get at them."

"Wow, that's terrible," the young teacher lamented. "I can't believe he would take it that far!"

"I know, it's a tough one. And we're going to do our best to shoot down any accusations against you in the press; Jason was extremely cooperative, and corroborated your story to the fullest," he smiled, "So, congratulations. I think you two really have a chance."

"Thanks," she shifted anxiously, "I appreciate all your help." Moving towards the door, she felt as if the two of them had been separated long enough. "Come on guys; it's time for you to meet…" her voice trailed away, not exactly sure what to call him; *he's so many things to me.*

Entering his room, the group kept their voices down, noting that the young man lay in a half reclined position. His eyes closed, he appeared to be resting, but he opened them as soon as they came in, greeting them with a weak, "Hi."

Moving around to the far side, Becky grasped his hand, "Hi." Making the rounds, she introduced everyone, an anxious grin growing on her face.

"Nice," Jason nodded. "Glad to finally put some faces with the names."

"She told you about us?" Luke appeared skeptical.

"Oh, yeah. Back when we were dating, she talked about you non-stop. Really made me wish my family were as close-knit as yours," he admitted quietly.

"Well, son," Matt reached over and gave his foot a squeeze through the blanket, "Your family is as close-knit, now that you're a part of it!"

Shaking her head slowly, Becky sighed. Not sure if she needed to laugh or cry, her emotional rollercoaster had left her exhausted. Taking in her mother, her brothers, and the love of her life, she had to admit things were looking up, and with any luck; they would stay that way.

Epilogue

BECKY SHIFTED NERVOUSLY, smoothing her dress; "I still don't think I should have worn white."

"Nonsense," Karen scolded. "That's an outdated tradition. Every princess should wear white on her special day."

"Yeah," the girl agreed, taking in the full length mirror one more time. "He does treat me like one, doesn't he?"

"You bet he does," the other woman giggled. "And not just because he's rich."

"Shh," Rebecca warned, "You know he hates to talk about money. I can't believe his parents went that far to try and run me off; pretending to disown him."

"Well, it don't matter and never did," Karen agreed. "I think you're set. You want me to go and check on Tanner?"

"Yes, please. And send mom in."

"Will do," she slipped out the door to look in on Becky and Jason's son.

Standing alone in the tiny room, waiting for the time to make her way out front, she thought about her wedding day. "June sixteenth; the anniversary of our first date," she commented to herself. It had been two years since their first outing; "I'm glad we waited; both times."

Her mind drifting to her father, she dabbed at a tear, sad that he had not lived to see it. "It's ok, daddy; Matt's going to walk me down the aisle."

The door opened and her mother entered, dressed in a beautiful lavender gown. "Are you ready, baby?"

"Yes, momma; almost," she reached for a wrinkled hand. "I wanted to talk to you first, for just a second." Becky swallowed hard, then cleared her throat a few times. "I wanted to thank you for being so patient with me. I wasn't ready for this, for a long time. I was selfish, and didn't have room in my life for a husband or a family."

"Aww, baby," her mother smoothed her hair. "We all grow up in our own time. I knew someday you'd find the one. I'm sorry I pushed you, an' tried to make you rush."

"It's ok," she shook her honey waves and pulled her veil over her face. "I'm ready. And I'm so glad that I waited for Jason."

About the Author

Anyone who knows me could tell you, I am a friendly kind of person, never met a stranger and take up conversations anywhere at any time. I work hard, and my mind never seems to shut down, as I wake up often in the middle of the night with ideas pouring out and demanding to be dealt with. Of course that means much of my books were written in the middle of the night.

I grew up and still live in the great state of Texas where everything is bigger, where we have warm weather and a central location. I love my state, my town, and my family, which includes my four sons, my significant other, and many friends as well.

I have thoroughly enjoyed writing this story and hope that you will love reading it just as much. And of course, there will be many more adventures to come.

You can follow Samantha Jacobey at:
Website: www.SamJacobey.com
Facebook: https://www.facebook.com/SamJacobey
Twitter: https://twitter.com/SamJacobey
Pinterest: http://www.pinterest.com/samanthajacobey/

Also by Samantha Jacobey

Summer Spirit Series - no one EVER had a summer romance like this… Charlie visits another plane, parallel to our own, where Summer Angels and Dark Angels battle over the fate of man. A unique twist on an old idea that will keep you guessing; will Charlie and Clarisse ever find their HEA? (New adult)

Irrevocable Series – from affluent beginnings, BAILEY DEWITT's life has become a broken mess... after her parents died unexpectedly, she didn't think it could get any worse. But when the arrogance of man catches up and puts the entire world into a dooms-day spiral, there will be only ONE PLACE she can run to... the ONE PLACE she wanted desperately to escape.... (New Adult)

Teach Me to Prey – in this standalone thriller, JASON TRUITT and his friends have gotten their way for years. Deceit, sex, and foul play aren't normally covered in the curriculum, but they're doing whatever it takes to get under BECKY STEWART's skin. When one of the boys turns up dead, it's a race against time to save the others; a STUNNING STORY that will get your heart racing and leave you breathless by the end… (New Adult)

The Wicked Awakened – a Halloween novel, a five hundred year old witch wants to turn SARAH MATTHEWS' body into her new home… A twisted tale involving a coven hell bent on seeing that she succeeds. Who will come out on top in this epic battle of wills? (Mature read, 18+ for sexual content and violence)

Also from the Lavish Family

The Norn Novellas

A. Nicky Hjort

http://myBook.to/NornNovellas

The Norn Novellas are all chapters in the epic saga of the youngest and most fickle of the four Norn Sisters. The same feisty immortal creature who must escape her inherent inner darkness to learn the meaning of life.

Each story takes a classic fairytale and spins it on its head, as we learn that maybe Norse Mythology was so much more than legend. And to think, you thought you knew those old tales so well.

Meet Za and find out what really happened...

When Tundra Turns to Ardnyt - Book 1: In the center of a magical world there grows a beautiful and terrible chasm of climbing plants. On one side of the Ivy Wall we find the hell-of-Tyndra, on the other, the heaven-of-Ardnyt. But legend has it that in the middle...lives a preternatural beast that imprisons and tortures the children from both sides.

When the war against time begins, Azza will have to cross over the Ivy Wall, something that has never been done before by a living being. But if she does make it through, she just might discover who she really is and how she became trapped in this alternate reality.

A fairytale at heart, this is the first chapter in the epic saga of the youngest and most fickle of the four Norn Sisters. The same feisty immortal creature who must escape her inherent inner darkness to learn the meaning of love.

A veritable palindrome from start to finish, the narrative of Where Tyndra Turns to Ardnyt journeys through duality to discover what shocking truths emerge when up becomes down, life becomes death, suffering becomes release, and the most unexpected endings become the most surprising beginnings.

Welcome to a place where forwards and backwards are exactly the same direction. Here Where Tyndra Turns to Ardnyt.

Where Ebon Sounds Like Ivory – book 2: Norse legend has it that the arms of the Yggdrasil tree—a sacred instrument of Odin—are ever-reaching, and its survival is necessary for life itself to continue.

During Winter's Solstice, when the search for her mortal mother begins, Za will have to cross over the Ebon Branch of the Dead—a feat that has supposedly never been survived intact. But if she does make it across and back home, she just might discover why she and the other three Norn Sisters of Fate came to be.

A fairytale at heart, this is the second chapter in the epic saga of the youngest and most fickle of the four Norn Sisters. The same feisty immortal creature who must discover her true origins to understand her inherent inner darkness. Only this way can she learn the meaning of unconditional sacrifice in the name of impenetrable love...when, as her destiny would have it, all the branches of such a powerful tree tremble treacherously in her tiny little hands.

A veritable unraveling of Snow White, the narrative of Where Ebon Sounds Like Ivory journeys through the most horrible of realms where shocking truths emerge. Here where death mimics life, obsession masquerades as devotion, and the most unexpected endings become the most surprising beginnings of a classic tale. One...you thought you knew so well.

Welcome to a place where the darkest of melodies births a miraculous tune of surrenderance. Here Where Ebon Sounds Like Ivory and Christmas, as we know it, begins.

Behind Blue Eyes Series
Sara J. Bernhardt
http://mybook.to/BehindBlueEyesSeries

A father's desire to save his child presents him with an unthinkable choice that leaves him darker than human, forced to roam through time alone as he searches for the place he belongs.

Adam Gold – Book 1: Fleeing the French invasion of Geneva Switzerland in the 1700s, Adam Gold books passage to America with his family. On the ship, Adam's daughter falls fatally ill. A mysterious man comes to Adam with a way to save his child by turning Adam into something darker than human.

The Medallion – Book 2: Adam Gold, an immortal with sweet eyes of blue, rushes through the centuries on a quest for reason and a thirst for revenge. To cope with his pain and regret, he sleeps away the years and awakes in a new era with a powerful, ancient vampire who sets her sights on him.

Golden Shackles – Book 3: When the ancient queen, Sekhmet snatches up Adam, he is faced with a terrifying decision. To help aid her in her vile plans or dare to stand against her.

Plus 3 more segments!

www.ingramcontent.com/pod-product-compliance
Lightning Source LLC
Chambersburg PA
CBHW020416150626
46554CB00014B/1874